Dirty RIDE

Dirt Track Dogs: The Second Lap Book 2

P. JAMESON

DIRTY RIDE

P. Jameson
www.pjamesonbooks.com

Published in the United States of America

First Digital Publication: March 2017
First Print Publication: April 2017

Formatting and Cover Design: Agent X

DEDICATION

For the readers who loved Drake and Ella, Beast and Punk, Blister and Annie, Surge and Tana, and Diz and Destiny enough to ask for more. I've loved growing the Dirt Track Dogs pack with you. Thank you for giving these rascally characters a chance, and for sticking with me through their stories..

ACKNOWLEDGEMENTS

These books wouldn't have been possible without the help of Team PJ. You might be silent, but you are powerful behind the scenes. You know who you are, and I could never thank you enough for standing by my side, lending a shoulder to cry on, and schooling me on where to put commas. To my mister and my little pack-monsters: you are my greatest inspiration. Thank you for supporting me and making sure I'm fed and watered. And for bringing me homemade little gifts to make me smile during deadline (looking at you Big Boo). I love you, my family. To my alpha friend: you have been there since the beginning, holding me up, pushing me forward, cheering me on. Putting up with my crazy days, my insecurities, and my horrible auto-corrected messages. I don't think I've ever been able to express what that means to me. Especially the last part. Just kidding. I love you, my friend.

And finally, to my readers, you amazingly magical motherfluffers: you have pulled me up out of the gutter more times than you know. Your sweet messages and reviews. The personal stories you've shared with me. All of your support just blows me away. Each and every one of you have taken part in this ride with me, and we still have so many miles left! You have found my books and loved them and pushed them to the top, and it means more to me than I even have words for. You are the stars in my eyes. You are the rubber on my tires. You are extraordinary.

ONE

"Mmm. Mmm. Mmmmm." Sally Davis hummed in appreciation as the fine, fine male specimen pushed through the door of Red Cap Bar & Grill looking like sex on a stick she wanted to lick. He'd be candy apple flavored. Because he always smelled like apples. Even under all that grime and grease he was covered in sometimes.

Not tonight though. Tonight he was scrubbed clean. Jeans that were the perfect amount of holey, and a fresh white t-shirt under that leather jacket.

Her inner vixen purred. "Will you look at that,

ladies. Look what the cat dragged in."

Three heads turned for the door. Barb, Seraphina, and Ragan. The fourth stayed focused on her drink. Lexington was taken. Like, lay you out on a table and bang you to New Zealand and back taken. She had zero point zero interest in anyone other than her human mate, Aaron.

As it should be. But still, it was taking some getting used to.

"Who? Rider?" Ragan asked, skeptically.

"Yeah, Rider. You gotta admit, he's the hottest male in town."

Her girls stayed silent.

"I'm not the only who thinks so, right? *Right?* He's an easy ten on the Dick-ter scale."

"I dunno," Seraphina murmured as her gaze found another male. "You sure there isn't an eleven out there somewhere?"

"I told you, peach. No such thing as an eleven."

But her hopeful gaze remained glued to Hot Rod Turner, the county's local radio DJ, where he stood over by the juke box. He wore a Van Halen t-shirt with the arms cut off, a backwards ballcap, and on his feet... camo Converse sneakers. The man never wore the same Converse twice. Sally would bet on it. He was scruffy, but he always had a grin and he was down to party.

Still. He wasn't hot like Rider was.

"They all suck," Barb groused uncharacteristically. "Alllll the males in this town. The only reason I even stick around is because of you bitches."

"Not true," Ragan argued. "You stick around for Mac too." Mac, the man who'd taught them everything they knew about motocross. "And Old Man Hubbard. And the dogs. And all those little young everybody around here has."

"Yeah." Sally nodded. "You just mad because you can't get a two word conversation out of Adam." The guy wasn't the friendliest, and Barb had taken a liking to him. He stood chatting with Rod, still in his work uniform, complete with an oval name patch above the breast pocket.

Uniforms could be hot.

Leather jackets and smirky brown eyes were hotter.

"And because Rod won't play your song on the radio."

Barb pouted. "He says it's not classic rock. How much more classic can you get than *Proud to be an American*? Huh? You tell me that."

Lexington tipped her beer bottle up for a gulp before answering. "I think he takes issue with the whole 'rock' part of classic rock."

Barb frowned harder and Sally kept waiting for her trademark stupid-happy grin to show up. Barb was an optimist's optimist. She bright-sided the hell outta life. But lately, she wasn't quite pulling off the happy-go-lucky feel.

"Proud to be an American is totally... like, *totally*... a rock song."

"It's not," Lexington said flatly.

"It is. Watch."

Barb kicked back her chair and stepped onto the seat. The song that was playing on the old juke box in the corner came to a twangy halt and the slow, proud riffs of a new song started. Barb cleared her throat extra loudly and found Hot Rod Turner across the room where he nursed a Heineken.

"Oh, you have got to be kidding me," Sally muttered, looking around the bar to see what kind of damage this might do to her reputation. But naw. It was kind of already in the shitter. And they'd only been in Cedar Valley a couple months.

She smiled to herself.

Sinful Sally worked fast. Got around good.

That's right, Sally girl. Make 'em talk, her inner fox purred.

People talking was exactly what she wanted. No male fox shifter would fight, as they liked to do, for a defiled female. Which meant no suitors would come sniffing for her. Which meant no one would die trying to earn the rights to her.

Unfortunately, it also meant she'd never have anything deeper than physical with a man. She'd never have what Lexington and her mate Aaron had. True love, beautiful and real and sweeter than a cherry cordial. There would be no soul-mate connection. No young for her to bear. No family besides her girls and their brand new pack family, the Dirt Track Dogs.

She'd be alone forever.

The familiar ache of loneliness rolled up from her chest to clamp around her throat. It was a vicious chokehold. One she experienced more and more these days.

She'd never wanted this life. She used to twirl around in fucking princess dresses and dream of a fairytale mating. She would have a strapping, handsome prince who would sweep her off her feet. They'd have three kits, each a year apart. Two boys and a girl, if her wishes came true. And they'd live happily ever after.

It was only what every girl deserved.

But her dreams came crashing down when her best friend, Ragan, was thrust into a fierce battle for her freedom. Five hounds sniffed her out. More than any other female in the history of their small skulk. Five males wanted to claim her.

Five males fought to the death for her, as was their custom. Funny how no one told Sally about that ritual when she was gushing about her fairytale happily-ever-after.

Bastards.

The meanest motherfucker won Ragan even though her fox had chosen another, and she was given over to him, her protests ignored.

Sally closed her eyes remembering the sound of Ragan's horrified screams as the asshole dragged her off to his den. She was barely of age. Barely more than a young, with a body more buxom than her years. She was with young in a matter of days and the horror that followed, was what banded the vixens together and led them to Cedar Valley and the Dirt Track Dogs seeking a safe haven.

Found it, they had.

Safety. It was a nice fucking change. But it wasn't enough to convince Sally she was truly safe from a claiming. From being a pawn in some male's macho quest. From being the cause of useless murder to determine who was the best male to have her. It was brutish and archaic and she'd rather fuck every male on earth once than risk being tied to one who only wanted to own her.

Her choice to be as dirty as possible meant she couldn't have love. Well, fine. It was worth it to have a clean conscience. To have no one's blood on her hands. To keep the hounds away. To be free.

The loneliness was worth it, even if she could never let things get farther than a one night stand.

But...

She glanced around the bar, taking inventory.

...she'd have to go slow through the guys in Cedar Valley. It was a small town.

Barb belting out the end of the first verse of the famous Lee Greenwood song brought her attention back around.

The wiry vixen had one hand pressed to her chest just above her glittery pink tube top as she stared down a smirking Rod and sang, "and you can't take that awaaaaaaay. Because I'm proud to be an American, where at least I know I'm free..."

Sally slid a little lower in her chair, but to her surprise, Seraphina, the sweetest and quietest of the vixens, kicked her own chair back and climbed up next to Barb. "And I won't forget the men who died, who gave that right to me," she sang, looping her arm around Barb's neck and narrowing her gaze at Rod.

"What the hell is happening here?" Sally hissed.

"And I'll gladly stand *up*—next to you, and defend her still today..."

Ragan and Lexington raised their drinks to the two crooning vixens, and one of them was humming loudly. Barb raised an expectant eyebrow at Sally.

"Aw, hell no." Sally shook her head. "I'm not doing this." She glared at Lexington who was sneaky chuckling. "You started this. You argued with her."

"There ain't no doubt I love this laaaaaaand.

God bless the USAAAAAA!"

The bar erupted in cheering even though there was still a whole verse left of the song.

"See!" Barb hollered over at Rod.

Sexy, sinful Rider had joined him. He leaned against the wall, one leg pulled up cooler than fucking James Dean.

"That rocked, Hot *Bod* Turner. In fact, it *fucking* rocked. It rocked so much I'd say it even rolled. And you know what they say, if it rocks and it rolls..." Barb shrugged, splaying her hands and tipping her head sassily to one side to swivel her shoulders. "... then it's a rock song, baby."

The Red Cap patrons, all in differing states of drunkenness, cheered again.

Rod shook his head, a genuine laugh rolling from his throat. When the noise died down, he drawled, "It's Rod. Hot *Rod* Turner. And... not playin' it, princess. You can croon all ya want, but that song right there? It ain't getting played on my *classic rock* radio station. No. Naw. And hell naw."

Sally's attention was on Rider though. He

nodded his head in agreement, dark hair falling slightly over his haunted eyes, and tapped the neck of his beer bottle to Rod's as if it sealed the words, like some king's insignia.

Barb frowned hard. She didn't like to lose. None of them did. That went for on the race track *and* in every single matter of life in general.

"I'll race ya for it," she called across the growing din of everyone getting back to their drinks. But her clear sharp voice, cut through it, bringing everything back to silence.

She had their attention. There was nothing Cedar Valley citizens loved more than a good race. On the dirt track, mostly, but they'd cheer their asses off for a three-legged foot race just as hard as they would at the speedway.

"Race me?" Rod chuckled as if Barb was off her rocker, but Sally could see she'd snagged him. What blue-blooded small-town guy could turn away a throw-down like that.

Barb nodded, still standing on her chair, hands ringing her hips at the waist of her low-slung jeans. "On the dirt, you and me. I win, you play this *insanely* wonderful song on the morning show on the day of my choosing."

His lazy smirk took up his entire face as he found his boys. They'd all joined him and Rider. Aaron, Lexington's mate, who's laughing gaze hadn't left her once. And brooding Adam, who was studiously ignoring Barb.

That man was a mystery. He wasn't like the others. He didn't play. Someday, someone was going to have to bust up all his concrete walls and make him smile. Sally would call that event the Smilepocalypse because it would also be the day the world ended.

Poor Barb.

"And if I win?" Rod countered.

Barb considered his question. "You win, you name it. Whatever you want. Month supply of Annie's cheesecake? Drinks for a year? Your call."

He narrowed his eyes, rolling his tongue over his front teeth in contemplation before seeming to come to a decision. He'd probably go for the cheesecake. Annie's cheesecake was orgasmic.

"I don't race bikes," Rod muttered dismissively. "And you don't race cars. Sorry, babe."

Seraphina scowled and jumped down from her chair, bringing her drink to her lips and chugging it down. Sally noticed the hint of fox eyes in her gaze. Huh. The vixen was close to turning. Interesting since out of all of them, she had the tightest control of her animal.

The sound of disappointment flickered through the room in a wave of, "aww."

But Barb wasn't so easily deterred. "Someone can race in your proxy."

"My proxy?"

"Sure, why not. How about Sally? She's on your side in this matter anyway. She's damn near anti-American if you ask me. Anti-good music at the very least."

The hell?

Sally frowned. "Am not. I'm wearing American flag panties right this very moment. It's a stars and stripes paradise down there. *And* I got dressed to Alanis Morissette. Fuck you very much."

Barb raised her eyebrows in appreciation.

"Yeah. So there."

"Alanis Morissette is Canadian though."

"And damn good music. So move along, bitch."

When Sally looked away, her gaze tangled with Rider's fiery hot one.

Well hello there, desire. Nice to meet you.

Fucking hell. The way his eyes were eating her up made her go instantly molten between her legs. His gaze melded to her body like it wanted to become one with it, sliding over every curve and valley. And when he reached her hips and stayed there, something made her slide lower in her chair and spread her knees. Like the wanton woman she was.

You want to see them, don't you? My panties. And what's underneath. You want to have your own personal little fourth of July with little Sally. Don't you?

She licked her lips, images of him cradled in the valley of her thighs making her skin flush even hotter.

"I stand corrected," Barb quipped, reminding Sally she and Rider weren't alone and splashing cold water all over her horny vibe. "But she still doesn't like my song. So what do you say, Hot Shot Turner, DJ of Cedar Valley's favorite morning show. Let Sally race in your place?"

"How do I know she won't lose on purpose?"

Sally's gaze snapped away from Rider and leveled on Rod.

"Don't make me hurt your face. I never lose on purpose."

She stood and strolled over to stand right in front of the human.

"In fact, I *never* lose… I only run out of gas and laps." The wild Dirt Track Dog named Surge taught her that one. Sure, the werewolf was half a fry short of a pancake, but he said things that got a person thinking. She considered him her

Smartass Mentor. "And tricks." She added the last part as a nod to her motocross days, and smiled to herself.

Damn, she was a fine smartass apprentice.

The place filled with hollow *ohhhhhs* and *damns* and *did-she-justs* as the throw-down landed right where it belonged… at Hot Rod's feet.

He glanced at Rider since he was the closest. And yeah, Sally was so aware of his nearness she was practically vibrating.

Rider tipped his head, a *you're in trouble* smirk playing at his lips. "Gotta do it, man. Can't let that challenge go unanswered. How will you ever show your face around here again?"

"Aw, shiiiit," Rod cursed, and knowing chuckles rose from the patrons listening. "Fine, fine. We race. Tomorrow night at dusk."

"Woooo hooo!" Barb clapped her hands together and jumped from her chair, doing some weird dance that made her look like a chicken.

Sally nodded, giving Rod her best shit-eating grin. "We race. Bring something to wipe your tears, yeah? Because I'm going to make you *weep* for doubting me."

TWO

Sweet Jesus. Rider swallowed hard, the gulp he'd sucked from his beer bottle somehow sliding past the knot of desire in his throat. There was absolutely zero things sexier than a woman who could make threats like that and back them up with her actions.

Sinful Sally they called her, because she was unapologetic in her ways. Her bluntness, her sexiness, her smartass mouth. And he had no doubt she could legit make Rod, a full grown, burly, blue-blooded man, cry real tears.

She was smokin' hot.

And she knew it.

Dangerous combination.

She strutted back to her friends, wagging her perfectly peachy ass as she went. It was the fox in her. It made her move like a glorious little temptress.

Yeah, the vixen was dangerous. And not just because she was part animal under all that deliciously lithe human body. She was dangerous because for the first time in a very fucking long time, Rider felt… interest.

In a woman.

For reasons other than screwing her brains out for a few hours in order to relieve his ache for closeness, and distract him from the way his heart still hurt.

Sally was a curiosity he couldn't shake. And he'd damn well been trying to for several months already. There were so many things he needed answers for.

Like what did her hair feel like? Was it as soft as it looked. Like gold satin.

Why did she talk to everyone like she already knew them? Like she was an old acquaintance. A buddy who was just shootin' the breeze.

What made her walk like she owned the opposite sex? Like she commanded them. She blinks, they drool. And what made her sometimes lose all that confidence as if she was two entirely different people.

Would her smile always be a sarcastic smirk? Or was there something that could make her smile for real. Wide and free. Absent of all the smartassity.

Shit, what would her mouth taste like? Her skin be like? Her legs around his waist, her fingers in his hair? Her moans in his ear? Her nails in his back, her eyes when she came, her smell…

The questions never stopped.

Which was why he could never get too close to her. That was a big hell naw.

Rider lived by a one-night only rule. And she was too intriguing for one night to be enough.

Maybe this time it's different.

A sick feeling wrapped around his gut as ancient memories swamped him. Memories of a time he was happy. Memories that should have been sweet but were only a nauseating shadow over his present. When he'd had everything he ever wanted. When he was faithful to a woman he loved harder than anything else in the world.

And man alive, did it cost him.

Cost him everything.

He'd never give another person that much of his soul again. He couldn't. Wouldn't.

No matter how she captured his attention.

Conclusion: Sinful Sally was off limits. Forever.

Sighing, he scanned the room looking for tonight's distraction. Hunting. Prowling. For the perfect lady who wouldn't expect anything more than a few hours of pleasure.

It was easy mostly. Find the one that looked lonely. Like he was. If the loneliness matched, it worked for him. It was something he could fix. Like the bikes in his shop. He knew how to make the loneliness go away for a night, and he liked being able to do that for someone else too.

But as he looked around, no one seemed to fit the bill.

No one had for a while now, and it was damn inconvenient for his cock.

The bar was busy as it always was on Friday night. People were laughing, pairing up, pool shooting, drowning in good food and beer. Happy. The air in the room was happier than it had been in past months.

Where the hell were all the lonely people like him? The ones drowning sorrows and shit. Even fucking Adam wasn't his normal broody self. He *was* broody. Just not as much as normal. And he was here at least, trying to have fun. Instead of holed up at home.

Was this some dumbass trick of the moon or something? The tides making people feel good? A witchy spell?

Witches existed, so it wasn't that far out. He knew that now. Like he knew about shifters.

There was even a sorta-vampire roaming the earth somewhere. Angels? Well, no one could answer that one for him yet. Aliens? Same thing. But he took no mythical creature for granted. Not after he'd watched goddamn Barb transform from a woman into a snarling, yipping fox when she'd thought Ragan's tiny son was in danger.

The boy was safe, of course. And the alpha of the Dirt Track Dogs had almost shit a brick when he realized humans they'd known for ages, raced with, bar-b-cued with, now knew their secret.

Huh. How'd he think it felt finding out your friends were werewolves? Not just wolves. Werecats and werefoxes. There was even a werefalcon up north somewhere. And werebears in central Arkansas.

Yeah, absorbing that information had been a bucket o'crazy. Talk about shitting a brick. Life hadn't been the same for any of them since.

His boys, Aaron and Rod, had all been acting like it was no big deal, and maybe it wasn't. But it sure felt like one. And if it wasn't such a big deal, why the hell hadn't they told Adam about shifters yet. Why was he the only one of them still in the dark?

Rider watched Aaron push off from the wall and join his new... well, *mate* was the word for what Lexington was to him. She wasn't just a girlfriend. Not a wife either. The bond they had was something deeper. Something Rider didn't understand at all.

It was forever.

She'd never leave Aaron, and he'd never leave her.

Or so they said.

But what made her stay? What made him so sure? Where were their guarantees.

Rider liked guarantees when it came to giving someone everything.

Aaron bent and dropped a kiss to the top of her head and when she looked up at him, he gave her a smile so private, it seemed wrong to be watching. But Rider didn't look away. If these two wanted privacy, they shouldn't be in the middle of a busy bar.

Aaron pulled a chair over to join the ladies and they went to bantering.

"Those girls," Adam muttered, shaking his head as he fingered the rim of his tall glass. "They're trouble."

Rider's gaze flicked to Rod and they shared an uncomfortable look. They hated keeping the vixens' secret from a person they trusted like Adam. But the DTD alpha, Drake, had asked them to give it time.

"Nawwww," Rod drawled. He was already getting a little loose. Rider guessed he was about four beers in and maybe riding a couple shots.

Rod drank too much. It was his go-to numbing agent. And yeah... they all liked to numb out. But Rod seemed to need to forget every damn thing before morning. If not, he was a mess for work. Rider wondered what Hot Rod Turner's morning show would sound like if he was sober.

"They ain't bad. They just a little gamey."

Adam frowned. "Gamey?"

Rod stumbled the short distance to the table Adam occupied and slumped into a seat. Rider followed.

"Yeah. Gamey. Wild, you know? Those ladies are *wiiiiiiild*. That's all."

Adam stared at him a little too knowingly. "How would you know exactly?"

Rod shrugged. "You can tell by watchin' em. Ain't no secret."

Adam grunted out a response and tipped his glass back for a drink. "Yeah well… I wonder when they'll leave. I'd rather them just be gone. Don't like how they're disrupting things."

"Gone?" Rod frowned hard, looking more serious than he had in a long time. "They ain't going anywhere."

Adam sat back in his chair, kicking his feet out in front of him. "Again, how would you know exactly?"

Yeah. Rider wanted to know that too. That thing about guarantees and all.

"Because," Rod snorted, as if that was enough

of an answer. But when Adam kept staring, waiting for more, he continued. "They've made a home here. At the motel, helping Old Man Hubbard. They get along swell over there. And... and at the race track. They got old Waldo to build a few jumps. That means they're important. Right, Rider? He ain't gonna revamp the track for just nobody."

Rider nodded reluctantly. Uncle Waldo did seem pretty fond of the vixens. But all that could end if he ever figured out they weren't quite human.

"And they're part of DTD now. Racing for the club. They've made themselves at home in Cedar Valley. Why the hell would they leave?"

Adam's questioning gaze turned dark. Like a shadow falling over a mountain as a storm rolled in. His voice was just as dark as he rumbled, "Everyone leaves."

Rider swallowed hard, knowing he was right.

"One way or another... everyone always leaves." Adam stood, dropping some cash on the table. "I'm outta here. Gotta pick up Megan."

Rider knew good and well Adam's daughter, Megan, was spending the night with Gracie at the DTD property. But if he needed to use her as an excuse to leave, who would stop him. It was a damn miracle he'd stuck around this long.

They watched him stalk from Red Cap and that age-old sadness settled in Rider's bones. He hated seeing all his friends so fucked up. Aaron was on the mend, but the rest of them were shit just barely making it. If things didn't start looking better soon…

Rod flicked his hand in the air, getting the waitress's attention for a refill. "They ain't leavin'," he muttered as if Adam was still there to argue with.

"They might."

Rod twisted his head to glare at Rider. "They made a pact with the wolves. They wanted a place to call home. A place to be safe from their shitty foxy people. They have it here. Why would they leave?"

He made a good argument. But time had shown them all Adam's way was truth.

Rider supposed time could prove Adam wrong too. It was possible.

"Just be careful," he warned.

He wasn't sure about Rod's obvious attachment to the group, wasn't sure which vixen had piqued his interest, but he knew his friend couldn't take another let-down. He'd had too many in recent years. Another would break him good.

"Nahhhh," Rod slurred loudly. "Careful's for pussies, man. Careful sucks assballs and nipplemuffs. You know when I'll be careful, Rider? Huh?"

Rider rolled his eyes, letting off a sigh. "When?"

Rod held his new beer up high, sloshing it over the side of the cup. "When I'm dead. That's when. 'Til then, call me daredevil Rod. Yeah?"

"Can't."

"Why not?"

"Because it sounds stupid as fuck, that's why."

Rod slurped his drink and Rider fingered the label on his bottle. This night was not feeling good.

"Huh." Rod nodded to himself. "Yeah, I think you're right. But still, the sentiment stands. Careful is for numb-nut losers."

"I'm careful, and my nuts aren't numb."

"Yet to be proven."

Rider blew out a breath, scanning the bar again for his mark. *Lonely, lonely where are you?* His gaze passed over so many ladies. One by one, he settled on them, and one by one, they felt all wrong. Until he landed on the fierce-eyed blond he'd been avoiding for the last fifteen minutes.

Sally.

She watched Lexington and Aaron, a skeptical smirk to her lips. She smiled at something Barb said. Passed the salt to Seraphina, and elbowed Ragan while some snarky or inappropriate comment slid past her tongue. But the thing that caught his attention... her smile didn't reach her eyes. It wasn't genuine. And even surrounded by her crew, by the laughing jibing group, she seemed alone.

Sally, who was steadfastly making her way around town the same as Rider was... was lonely. Lonely like he was. They were the same.

In fact, she was the only one in Red Cap that called to him. That might be able to calm that burn inside for tonight. Yet... he wasn't going to have her. Not her.

She looked over and caught his gaze, but he didn't look away. Should've. Fucking should've. But it was impossible. Those sexy blue eyes cut through the dim light of the room like laser beams. Framed by her slender cheeks, they were all he could see. A strand of hair hung over her forehead, and if he were closer, he might brush it out of the way. Or he might not. Hopefully he wouldn't.

Damn it.

He broke away, desperately scoping the bar again. But there was nobody for him. There was only one thing to do. He needed to leave. Go home. Sleep in his own goddamn bed. And it was a chump move, leaving Rod here by himself. He never did that. But maybe the guy would understand this time.

A whistle caught his attention and he jerked his head in the direction from which it came. Sally stood, one hip against the pool table, chalking a cue stick. Who knew that action could look so goddamn sexy.

"Let's play," she said. "Doubles. You, me, Rod, and Sera."

Rider didn't answer right away. Didn't look at Rod either.

"Come on," Sally urged, lazily popping her gum. "I'm bored. Save me. Be a hero right now, Rider Daley." But her eyes were calculating, giving her away. What was she up to?

Everything about her right then brought his every nerve ending to attention. The way his name sounded on her glossy lips. The challenge in her gaze. The way she leaned so casually against the table. How she wore her confidence like a robe to cover whatever darkness had made her seem empty. God, did she think she was fooling people?

She quirked one eyebrow, amping up the challenge.

Well, shit.

He could say no, and leave. But that would be caving. To her, to the pressure of his own expectations, to his failures, past and current.

He could stay, and play with Sally. Which sounded a whole hell of a lot better. And a hell of a lot more dangerous...

Decisions, decisions.

Rider eyed her. Staring right into him, she rested the stick between her curvy thighs, close—very close—to her sweet spot, and used a cue slicker to shine the shaft. Her grip was slow and steady.

And tight.

Up and down she went, her eyes never leaving his, her lips slightly parted in a sexy pout as her palm moved along the pole. On the last slow jerk, when she reached the top, she blew on the tip sending the excess chalk into the wind.

Fuck.

Rod said something but Rider didn't hear him. He was too preoccupied by the raging boner behind his zipper. Somehow, he'd felt every pump of her hands on the shaft directly in his fucking pants.

And that blow at the end… it was too real. The tip of his cock tingled from it. The sultry way her lips were parted, he could imagine his hands tangled in her silky hair as he guided his erection slowly to her mouth. He'd torture himself with how slow he went, easing past that swollen glossy opening to sink into the warm wet heat. She'd hum when he hit the back of her throat and he might not be able to go slow after that.

Rider stood from his chair, pausing to unashamedly adjust his obvious erection. No use in hiding that shit. She knew what she was doing.

He sauntered over, stopping too close to her. Close enough to smell her faint perfume. It was like telling secrets in the dark. Sweet and sharp, driving a new thread of desire right through his cock like a spire.

He took a swig of his beer and watched her eyes as they stayed on his mouth. Sally was a tall lady, but this close, he towered over her. And he used that to his advantage. If Sinful Sally wanted to play... well, he was a master at the seduction game. Question was, which of them would come out a winner. Him? Her? Both? Neither?

If he was betting, he'd put his money on that last one.

"Nice job polishing that shaft," he husked. "Do you shine balls too?"

Her pupils flared, and he almost stepped back as her eyes changed from human to something else. Animal. Fox.

It should've been frightening. Instead, it made his balls tighten and his dick grow even harder.

Hot. As. Fuck.

"Oh, balls are my specialty. I'm very good with balls." She tipped her head to the side, sending her blond hair tumbling over her shoulder. "You wanna see my rack? I'm a pro at getting balls in my rack."

Rider bit back a smile. Shit, this woman was his kind of humorous, turning all these pool terms into dirty talk.

"I'd love to see your rack, Sally." His eyes dipped down to where her tits threatened to pop out of the top of her tank-top. "I bet your rack is the stuff wet dreams are made of."

She smiled knowingly, spinning away from where he'd cornered her between his body and the billiard table. "It's settled then. I'll rack 'em, you break 'em. Sera, Rod! Let's go."

Rider drew in a tight hiss as she accidently—or not—brushed against his hips and tossed a saucy grin over her shoulder.

And in that moment, he truly didn't know which of them would prove better at this game. But fuck-all, they were playing it.

Yeah. They were playing it.

THREE

Rider came awake to the sound of hammering, before his eyelids could fully open. He lay on something soft, but not as soft as his own bed. And he'd been dreaming. Of sexy curves in his hands, a sultry scent in his nose. And sassy words in his ear. Sally…

Shit.

He struggled to open his eyes, pushing to a sit at the same time. Bright rays of light beamed in through a crack in the heavy drapes. But the room, the bed, was unfamiliar.

A whole lot of *oh shit* settled over him. He

never stayed until the sun came up. He never let morning find him in his flavor-of-the-night's bed. For both parties' sake, he left after a few hours. Usually after she fell asleep. It cut out the awkwardness of saying goodbye after sharing the lonely night.

The hammering nearby made it feel like his head had bricks instead of brains, and he pushed at the pain behind his eyes with the heels of his palms.

"Mother of fuck," he muttered.

"Nope. Just Ragan and Mac working on the roof repairs."

Hearing Sally's voice woke him up faster than a splash of ice water.

He turned to see her beside him on the mattress, bare legs tangled in the messy sheets. His gaze followed a path upward until it touched on the curve of her ass. American flag panties. Well, fuck him stupid. The sight was a hell of a lot hotter than he'd anticipated. Stars and stripes forever and ever, amen.

Swallowing hard, he continued up, gliding over her tank covered back, over her shoulders and neck until he reached her head.

Holy hot mess.

Ratted-to-hell hair crowned her head, and her makeup-streaked face was smushed into the pillow. Her eyes were closed but she clearly wasn't asleep.

Only her mouth moved as she murmured, "Don't be lookin' at me with disdain, Rider Daley. You caused all this. I normally wake up looking like a sweet fucking dream. But not after last night. Not after that party between my legs."

Oh. Fuck.

Oh, hell.

Aw, shit.

"Party?" he gulped.

Her eyes flew open but the rest of her remained still. "Yeah. Party." Her gaze rolled over him much like he'd just done with her.

"What party, Sally?"

She sat up, staring him down like a grandma

in church, while he dug back through his dull memories, trying like hell to recall what happened. The fact that her tits were poking against the white tank top, braless, weren't exactly helping.

"You don't remember?" she asked, incredulous.

Rider scratched his eyebrow. "It's a little foggy."

She tipped her head to one side, sizing him up.

"You don't remember a thing, do you?"

He said nothing.

"You don't remember how you made it purr?"

Again, he kept quiet, and her expression turned naughty

"Or how we went so fast and hard? And for so long? Goddamn it, Rider. I can't believe you don't remember." She threw her pillow at him, and he didn't even try to stop it from smacking him in the chest. "You promised me you weren't too drunk. You promised you'd remember what we'd shared!"

Holy shit. Just how far did they go last night? It couldn't have been what it sounded like. No way. He'd remember rocking Sinful Sally's world. He'd only been thinking about it for months. And fuck, how was he missing everything from the pool table on?

"Goddamn it, Sally. Tell me what happened last night."

She took her time wrapping her ratted gold locks into a bun on top of her head. Damn, that was cute.

"You really don't remember?" There was a touch of humor in her voice.

Cute or not, if she didn't clue him in fast, he was going have to resort to something nefarious.

Threats. But what would scare Sally into spilling the deets?

"I swear to god, woman…"

Something flickered in her eyes. Something wicked and a little animalistic. He'd noticed it before, with her and the other vixens. Aaron said it was their inner fox coming close to the surface.

Rider had to admit, it was hot as hell.

Like every fucking thing about her.

"You took me for a riiiide," she purred. "Or rather, I took you for one. It was good. Real good. It's a shame you don't remember it." Her tone was light, and she plopped back to the bed.

But her words hit him like a punch right in the soft spot beneath his ribs. It felt like all the air in the room had vanished. Like he was the piece of shit in a toilet bowl, swirling and swirling, getting closer to that drain.

In all his man-whoring days, he'd never fucked up this bad. Never was so drunk he couldn't remember banging his girl. And never was he drunk enough to bang one he cared about.

But then again, he'd never cared about one like he did Sally. Not since…

Evie.

"No." He dropped his head to his hands. "Fuck. I'm sorry, Sally. This wasn't supposed to happen."

Rider stood from the bed to pace the small

room. He was relieved to find he was still in his jeans. Except how the hell did he give it to Sally good with his jeans still on?

Shit, she must've been dipping in the dry-hump bastard pool if she thought jeans-on was good. *Real good*, in her words.

And he recognized where he was now. They were at Old Man Hubbard's place. The little motel on the fringe of town where the vixens lived and worked.

"Look, I can't remember any of it, and I'm damn sorry. I'm not that kind of asshole, okay. But we shouldn't even be in this mess. I never would've fucked with you. Not *you*. Never in a million years. What *the hell* did I drink?"

He found her gaze across the room. She was quiet, lying back against the pillow, eyes narrowed to mere slivers. She'd lost any hint of playfulness. But there was something else... she looked furious.

"Sally—"

"Jack Daniels. Many shots. Too many,

apparently."

Jack. Well that explained it. JD was his kryptonite.

Or she was.

Or both.

She stood, walking to the closet and yanked some jeans free from a hanger. Quickly, she jerked them on over her American flag panties. And then, like it was no big thing, she ripped her tank over her head and replaced it with a sporty half-shirt bra.

Rider was drooling even with her back to him. Just the fact that she was bare in his presence was a knife in his gut.

What had he done? He'd never be able to fix this.

"I was playing with you," she said low. "Taking a dig at you because you couldn't remember last night. But don't worry, Rider. You didn't *fuck with me.*"

"What?"

She twisted to face him, her expression

showing sadness just before the shutters came down to look like normal carefree Sally.

"We didn't fuck, okay? We did exactly what I said. We went for a long ride on your goddamn Harley. You were too drunk to drive so I drove. We took all the backroads. Watched the stars. It was fun. We cut up. We laughed. We ended up here. You wanted to see my stars and stripes panties, so I showed you. You passed out in the bed. I crashed next to you. We woke up to Mac's hammering. The end."

"Wait, we didn't…"

"No, asshole. We didn't. So you can quit your frimping and fretting. Your integrity is still intact."

Rider blew out a breath of relief so hard he went dizzy from it. He bent forward, hands on his knees, sucking in air to get steady again.

"Holy shit." A relieved laugh bubbled out of him. It was obscene but he couldn't help it.

He was so damn happy he hadn't screwed Sally and forgotten it. Used her for relief. Yes, she matched his lonely side, and maybe he could have eased her the way he did other ladies. But… damn it, Sally deserved better than him. She deserved what Lexington had. Someone who could give her the goddamn world. Give her his entire fucking heart, that's what Sally deserved.

And Rider wasn't that guy.

"It was a joke," he said, sobering a little.

"Yeah," Sally deadpanned. "Like your abs. Put a shirt on."

Rider frowned, collecting his shirt from the floor. "What's wrong with my abs?"

Sally eyed his middle. "My guess is too much beer and not enough sit-ups."

Rider looked down, flexing. There was plenty of definition there. Maybe not as much as those werewolves, or even Aaron. But he was doing just fine. He didn't need sit-ups. He flexed his abs enough when he was doing the dirty.

But he kept that part to himself and pulled his shirt on.

"Sally… I'm sorry. I didn't mean to—"

"What? Assume that I'd fuck you?"

"—get that drunk."

She shrugged. "You don't see me crying, do ya?"

No, but maybe she needed to. Maybe she was hurt, and covered it up so he wouldn't know.

Rider watched her pull on a muscle shirt. The front of it said *Sexy As Brappp* with two dirt bike tires where her tits should be.

"So... we went riding, huh? Where'd we go?"

"Took some shitty road with no name out to Devil's Bend."

"Hog Swallow."

She frowned. "Getting damn tired of your insults, Rider Daley."

He barked out a laugh, wishing there wasn't a bed between them. No, wait. The bed was a good thing. Otherwise, he'd be trying to touch her. Take his finger to the crinkled spot between her brows and try to iron it out.

"The name of the road is Hog Swallow."

"You're shitting me."

"Naw. I'm not."

"What the hell kind of name is Hog Swallow?"

He shrugged. "It's what we do in Arkansas. Give things ridiculous names so people think we're crazy. Toad Suck. Bald Knob. Possum Grape."

Sally crinkled her nose. "I'm feeling violated right now."

"Be glad you landed in Cedar Valley. Pretty safe as far as names go. We do have Hog Swallow Road though. There's also Sog Hallow. It runs along the river out by the DTD club."

Sally blinked. "Yeah, okay."

He was talking too much. Rider never talked this much. He just needed to know she was okay. And the more he talked, the more he could gauge her.

She slung her hands around her hips. "Well, since you're here, I'm calling in a favor."

"A favor?"

"Yeah. You owe me for getting you to a safe place when you were drunk off your ass last night. I took care of you. Plus, we really did have fun.

Even if you don't remember it." The pain creeped into her voice. He was getting better at detecting it, the little things that told him she wasn't as solid as she pretended to be. "So... hell yeah. You owe me."

Rider crossed his arms and narrowed his gaze. "Awright, peach," he murmured, stealing the nickname she liked to use on damn near everybody. He liked it. It suited her ass. "Tell me what you need."

She pressed her lips together, but it wasn't in the normal sex-drunk way she did when she was in full-blown seduction mode. This time it was more natural, and he wanted to catalog it in his mind to think about later.

"Follow me."

Anywhere, he almost said out loud. But he stopped himself just in time. Inside, his heart only felt sicker as he gave himself a metaphorical punch to the gut. *Do not feel more for her. You're already too deep.*

But his vixen was reeling him in like a hooked

fish. How would he survive her? And why was every woman his heart chose, something he had to survive.

A guarantee. That's what Rider wanted. When his heart chose a woman, he wanted to know he wouldn't be left bleeding on the floor.

But Sally *had* taken care of him last night. So he followed her out of the room, watching her ass sway in front of him the entire time.

FOUR

I'd never fuck with you. Not you. Not a chance.

Rider's words were like a sledgehammer behind Sally's eyes. Made her feel so small. Low.

Like she was a leper. Disgusting. Untouchable.

Yeah, that's what she'd been aiming for. A deterrent for the males of her kind. But Rider feeling that way about her stung more than it should.

And to think, they'd been getting along so well last night that she'd thought they could be friends. Not like she was with the other Dirt Track

Dogs or Aaron's buds. But like… *real* friends. Best friends. More like she was with her girls.

She was wrong though. She couldn't be friends, much less something more, with someone who looked down on her without even knowing her reasons.

Her fox recoiled at the memory of Rider's despair when he thought they'd slept together. It hurt, his reaction. It hurt fucking bad. But she'd never let him know it.

She'd just focus on the good parts of last night.

They'd flirted playing pool, and for the first time in a long time, she found herself laughing from her gut. The real kind of laugh that she hadn't felt in so long. So when he'd asked her to go riding, even though he was drunk off his ass, she'd said yes. Just to make that good feeling last a while longer.

His engine purring beneath her as they cruised under the midnight stars made her feel alive again. Something more than a shell. It made her feel safe from the past she'd ran from for so long. And her fox had liked spending time with him, liked the way he talked about the night sky like it was an artist's canvas.

Had it been worth it, even waking up like they had this morning? Maybe. If she could make the pain in her center stop throbbing.

Damn it. If love was a thing, she might've fallen in love with him out there under the stars, while he was drunk and she was totally not.

But she awoke to the real Rider. Not the one under the influence of alcohol.

And he was an asshole pretty much.

What a fucking shame.

Sally led Rider down the hall of identical doors until they reached the small front lobby. Seraphina was behind the front desk, dressed more proper than any of them had in a long time—dark jeans and flowing navy shirt that buttoned up to the collar. She laughed with Old Man Hubbard, who was much less professionally dressed, wearing overalls. He leaned on his cane, but his eyes sparkled at whatever he and Sera were chatting about.

As Sally neared, she realized the old man was talking about his late wife, Nancy, and she had to smile. He sure loved telling the vixens stories of his ornery old lady and the trouble they used to get into when they were just starting out. Sally would never tell a soul, but she secretly wished for that kind of romance. One that was as fun as it was passionate. As humorous as it was sexy. If the world were perfect and she could have had her princess dream, she would have wanted it to turn out like Old Man Hubbard's.

"Hey, OM," she greeted him, stopping at the counter. OM, short for old man. She'd coined it when they arrived, and it stuck. "How's it hanging?"

Old Man Hubbard looked up, mischief in his gaze. "Kinda gnarled, and not quite hanging, I'd say, Sally-girl. More so sitting there like a strange lump really."

Sally barked out a laugh at the old man's

humor, and Sera put her face in her hands, covering her exasperation.

He looked over at Rider. "This is what you got to look forward to, sonny. Just puttin' that out there so you ain't blindsided in fifty years or so."

"Noted." Rider smirked at the old man, but his eyes crinkled at the edges telling Sally he liked the jokes.

Old Man Hubbard nodded. "You wait and see what I say."

The phone rang, and Seraphina answered it. She rattled off some options in a pleasant voice Sally could never imitate. She'd tried one day when no one was around to work the desk. It hadn't gone well.

Seraphina went to clickety-clacking on the computer, booking a reservation.

"Sally-girl, how are we coming on that washer situation? You need me to call in the big guys from Little Rock to come fix it?"

She was hoping they wouldn't have to go that route. The industrial repair company from the city was going to be expensive. Not as much as buying a brand new machine, but still. It would set OM back a few bucks.

The motel wasn't doing well business-wise, but Ragan was working on some ideas to boost people's opinions of the place. She'd taken over the PR, and already, after only a couple months, things were looking better.

But they were still in the red, and Old Man needed that load taken off his frail shoulders.

"Trying to avoid that, OM," she murmured. "It's why Rider's here. He's gonna look at it and see if he can figure out the problem for us."

The old man's burly silver brows went up into his forehead. "That's mighty nice of you, sonny."

Rider shrugged it off. "No big thing," he said. "I owed Sally a favor."

"Ah," the old man nodded, and Sally gave him a scandalous look.

"I'm gonna have us out of the red before you know it." She gave the old man a wicked wink, and he blushed under all those wrinkles.

"Oh, Sally-girl. You be good, now."

"I don't know what you're talking about," she tossed over her shoulder, leading Rider toward the laundry room. "I'm *always* good."

Old Man Hubbard's hearty chuckle made her chest full as she swiped her key to unlock the door and held it open for Rider to follow her in.

"Good to see the old man smiling," he mused. "You ladies have really brightened the place up for him."

Sally nodded. "He's good people."

She walked toward the back of the small utility room and stopped in front of the trouble machine.

"This the one?" Rider asked.

"Yeah. I've worked on it for hours. Changed the belts. Replaced the washers. Still won't run a full cycle. It's old. Those new ones have computerized shit. But this one, I figured one of us could fix it since it's all nuts and bolts, and save OM some cash. It's gotta be close to fixing a bike, is what I was thinking. I don't know. Will you take a look?"

Rider nodded, frowning at the machine and rubbing his hands together like he was anticipating the grease he'd get on them. "Got tools?"

Sally pointed to a box in the corner, and he went to digging through it. In minutes, he had a wrench and was elbows deep in gears, twisting and clicking to ferret out the problem. She watched the way the muscles in his back tensed with the movement. The way his biceps flexed… he was sexy as hell. She'd always had a thing for the working men. The tough ones. Their calluses felt good on her skin. Reminded her nothing worth having came easy.

In her case, freedom from her skulk. The clear conscious of no one killing or dying for her. And the tradeoff was sullying herself.

Worth it, her fox insisted. And she knew the animal was right.

But… maybe if she hadn't slept with so many people, she could have her happily-ever-after now. Like Lexington. Their pact with the Dirt Track Dogs made them safe. But she was already too dirty to be treasured, wasn't she?

Her stomach threatened to heave as she watched Rider work.

I thought he was the one, the vixen whispered, burrowing under all Sally's self-loathing.

Goddamn it. Her fox wanted her to get honest right now, and it was bad timing with him here. But that was the real problem, wasn't it? She'd thought if anyone could understand her ho ways, it would be another ho. Even if he was a ho of a different variety. A ho is a ho is a ho.

Or so she'd thought.

I'd never fuck with you. Not a chance.

"So, tell me about last night." His silky-rough voice broke her sadness-spiral. She'd been going down fast too. Talking about their stupid night would be a welcome distraction.

"What's the last thing you remember?"

He grunted. "Flirting my balls off with you at the pool table."

"Yeah. We did that."

He glanced over his shoulder, frowning. "I remember laughing. And making you laugh." He ducked back under the cover of the machine. "Prettiest sound in the world."

It was so quiet she might've missed it if not for her sharp fox hearing. And still, she wasn't so sure she'd heard him *correctly*.

Prettiest could have been… pigliest?

"You bet Rod you could make me laugh before he could. Said, and I quote, 'Not the fake shit you used to rope men in either. It only counts if it's real'. I kinda didn't dig what you were implying there. Just saying."

"Well, I had to put that stipulation on it. Otherwise, where's the challenge? You laugh all the time, but you don't laugh for *real*."

He paid attention to the way she laughed? She didn't think anyone did that. Not even the girls.

"Last night, I did. So."

"Hm. Did I win?"

"Yeah," she confirmed grudgingly.

Rider chuckled. "What else? What happened after we left? I want to know everything."

Everything? Sally wasn't sure if she wanted to give him everything. It was kind of... precious... those moments where she laughed freely and felt her animal opening to him. He couldn't remember them, and they meant zero to him, so maybe she didn't want to divulge any of it.

"Think I'll keep those details to myself, thanks."

"Not fair. It was our first date and I can't even remember it. You gotta give me something."

First date. The words tugged at her heart and made her angry at the same time. Because they were like an electronica song. They sounded good but they didn't mean anything. And that wasn't very nice after the way he'd acted when they woke up.

"It wasn't a date," she bit out, and he slowed his cranking on the wrench.

Rider pulled the cover back for the motor, setting it aside. "Hand me that flashlight," he said quietly.

She passed it to him, deciding to give him what he wanted. She'd tell him about their night. After all, if she gave it away, it wouldn't mean as much.

Like her virtue.

Story of her fucking life.

"We went up to the falls and sat on the rocks. In the dark, with nothing but the stars as company. We watched the moon make its way across the sky. You asked me things about my fox. I answered you. You held my hand. I let you. It was all very stupid and wouldn't have happened if you hadn't been drunk. It didn't mean anything. And we'd be better off just forgetting it."

She slammed her mouth shut. Bad choice of words.

"Hm. One of us already did," Rider murmured, peering at the machine and moving some wiring out of the way. "That's the problem, isn't it?" He sounded bothered. Maybe even as bothered as she was.

"It's not a problem."

Rider grunted a disagreement. "I don't know if I can help you with this, peach. This looks like something Adam needs to peek at."

The human was a machinery mechanic at a nearby pipe factory. He was going to be her next call, but she figured she'd try Rider first since he was a tad more pleasant.

"I can call him for you, if you want," Rider offered.

"Yeah, could you? He don't seem to be sensitive to my wiles."

Rider frowned, rising to stand from his crouched position.

"You know. My sex-suasion. The ability to charm men into doing what I want. Isn't that how people see me?"

Rider smirked. "You *do* do that though."

"Hm. Sometimes."

"That what happen last night? You use your wiles to get me to let you drive my bike?"

"No. You handed that over willingly."

"You said I held you hand?"

She nodded.

"I don't do that, you know? With other ladies. I don't hold hands."

What was he trying to say? Was he calling her a liar?

"Well, you did. Now call Adam, will ya?"

Rider narrowed his gaze at her, but pulled his phone from his pocket and dialed up his friend.

Their chatter blurred to dull noise in Sally's ears.

The space of the laundry room was too small. She needed air. Rider was sucking the entire room dry and she couldn't find oxygen.

What is happening to me?

Her fox chuffed inside, uncomfortable with the *feelings* churning beneath her skin. Feelings. That was her problem. She was feeling too much. Last night all the emotions had been pleasant. But now they were rubbing her raw like sandpaper

Rider said his goodbye to Adam and shoved his phone back in his jeans.

"Good news. He's got a few minutes on his lunch break. He says he'll stop by. I promised him a beer next go 'round at Red Cap."

He crouched low again, digging around in the machine parts. She could feel the way the mechanics of the thing fed his soul. Rider loved fixing things. She could practically taste his excitement in the air.

She looked away, not wanting to watch him anymore.

The pressure was building inside her, and she was going to blow. She could fake being tough in public, but here in this tiny room with him... after the night they'd shared...

Nope. She was going boom.

"Is it because I'm a slut?"

His head snapped around, but she couldn't look his direction. Couldn't watch whatever he was thinking bleed through his eyes. She was better off without that memory sitting in her brain, mocking her.

"That why you got so upset when you thought

we'd slept together?"

"No, Sally." He stood, facing her, wrench in hand probably. But still, she just stared at the door, wishing she would walk out of it. "That's not why. And you're not a slut. You shouldn't say that."

She let off a humorless laugh. "Yes, I am. And I didn't say I was ashamed of it. Just wondering if that's why you acted like it was the bad news of a lifetime."

"That's not it."

"Right."

"Sally, if you only knew..." His voice was wispy-raw. It sounded like she felt on the inside, and it managed to pull her gaze from the exit to the floor at his feet. He tossed the wrench into the toolbox, washing machine forgotten.

"It's okay for you to sleep your way around Cedar Valley. It makes you a stud, right. But it makes me dirty. Makes me disgusting."

"That couldn't be farther from the truth."

She shook her head, turning to leave. She

needed out. Needed air. Needed gone.

"Let me know when Adam gets here."

But her fingers had barely grazed the handle when she found herself spun around. Rider yanked her right up to his chest, breathing like a bulldog as he stared down at her. Sally grit her jaw at his nearness, at the hard planes of muscle that pressed into her softer curves. They fit together well. She'd always known they would.

"Where do you think you're going?" His nose grazed along her jaw so carefully and he inhaled. Like… an animal scenting her. Oh, shit. That made her vixen hotter than asphalt on a hundred degree day. "And why do you smell like candy? Like sweet hard candy. Sally, why do you smell so much like my hopes and dreams?"

She pushed at his chest, but he didn't let go.

"Don't tease me, Rider. Don't be cruel. Last night was the first time I felt normal in a long time, and I can't—*won't*—let you play games right now."

"I'm not playing," he bit out, his words

sounding sharp as nails. "But damn it, I wish I was. I wish I could be just like you. Just… not care."

He brushed his thumb so softly along her cheek.

"Do I look like I don't care?" Her question was soft as a petal. She could hear the tears in it before she even felt them spring to her eyelids. She willed them back, far back. She couldn't cry in front of Rider. She didn't cry in front of anybody.

His gaze roamed all over her face, touching on all the pieces of her expression before he murmured, "No, Sally. You seem like you care a lot."

His shoulders sagged. He looked defeated.

"It's okay," she said, letting her voice go wry. She felt like fucking Elsa. Conceal don't feel. Don't let him know. "I'm good at pushing that shit back in. Don't you worry."

Rider grit his jaw so hard the muscle flicked. She had the incredible urge to lick it. Stupid. Her urges had the stupidest damn timing.

"You misunderstood my reaction this

morning."

She shook her head.

"I was glad we hadn't fucked because I don't want you to be just one in a million that I took to bed. Understand?"

Sally frowned. What was he saying?

"Sally..." He groaned pressing her body even closer, and something amazing changed in the air.

She dragged breath into her lungs scenting out the difference. She recognized it. Rider had smelled like this last night, when they played pool at Red Cap. When they'd flirted shamelessly.

He pressed a trembling kiss to her jaw. She noticed how he avoided her mouth. But somehow it seemed sweeter. It melted her. She didn't know what was happening right now, but it was like nothing she'd ever done before.

No man had held her like this, like Rider did right now.

"When I think of you with other men... it doesn't disgust me. It drives me *insane*. I want to stop you, take their place. But I can't do shit about it because I'm fucking broken, Sally. You understand? I see you strutting around looking like sex on wheels and it's all I want to do. Be with you. But I know it would only be once, and we'd be done. Because that's what I am. A one-and-doner. My heart doesn't have more in it than that. And I can't do that to you. Can't do that to me."

"Why?"

He stared at her like she'd lost her mind. "You want a one night stand?"

"No, I mean… why doesn't your heart have more to give?"

He looked away, thinking about how to answer. When he did, she could tell he was sharing something he wouldn't share with others. Something risky.

"I… I need guarantees, Sally. When I care for someone, I care hard. Too fucking hard for my own good. I need to know that they won't throw it all away on a chance for a modeling career or movie star dreams or whatever the hell they fancy."

That seemed pretty specific. Someone had hurt Rider badly. It made Sally want to let her claws out. Maybe dig them around in some bitch's face.

"I need to know our relationship matters. That they treasure it as much as I do. Because when I commit, I'm done. She has me. Heart, soul, and mind. I want the fucking same." He pulled away, jamming his hands in his hair. "Shit, this is not what I want to talk about with you. You shouldn't know this."

Inside, her vixen pawed, demanding she share something just as valuable. Just as risky, so Rider wouldn't be alone. As if this was a give and take.

"I've been hurt too." She said the words on a deep breath and when they were out, she wanted to pull them back inside.

Rider turned back to her, looking furious. "Who hurt you?" he demanded, and his protective edge was like candy to her fox. Oh, she might be all alpha-female on the outside, but inside, she rolled around in this dominant shit like it was butter and she was a hot roll. "Who, Sally? Tell me."

She shivered, trying to find a way to answer him.

"My skulk."

His shoulders tensed, fists clenching. But he knew the way foxes mated, the way the vixens had been hunted. What he didn't know was how all that had changed her. How it molded and sculpted her into what she was.

"They're the reason I... I..." She swallowed hard. She'd never had trouble saying what she wanted to say before. But now, with him... with things spilling out between them, making a messy pile of unsorted feelings that both of them had been avoiding for months, she was finding it difficult.

Goddamn it, Rider *affected* her. Made her feel more like her old self. The princess who'd dreamed of a happily-ever-after. Not a wanton woman who only desired a happy-for-now.

"They're the reason I've sullied myself. God, Rider. I've never told a soul this, and I swear *to fuck*, if it ever leaves this room, I will have your nuts for it." She didn't wait for him to agree. If he broke her trust, she'd show him no mercy. "I've spent my entire adult life *striving* to ruin my reputation. *Striving* to be a woman that any male fox would be disgusted by. It was my entire goal, and I used males who wanted to be used to get this way. Because... I couldn't bear to be responsible for a *spur*."

"What's a *spur*?"

"It's what we call it when hounds fight for rights to a female. But if I made myself unworthy enough... no males would ever fight for me. I wouldn't have their deaths on my hands. And I wouldn't belong to the most brutal of them all when it was finished. I would only belong to... me."

Tears welled in her lids, blurring Rider to a blob of color. *Don't let them fall, don't let them fall...*

Damn it.

One slid over the edge, and Rider became clear again.

She turned aside, dashing the traitorous wetness away. But he was right there again, too close, trying to hold her.

Pulling free, she put some space between them. "No. Please. Just… give me a second."

Wrapping his hands around his hips, he kept his distance, waiting for her to pull her shit together.

With a few deep breaths and sheer grit, she managed to get her emotions under control, even if by a lousy hair-thread. She let off a quick awkward laugh. "Your nuts, Rider," she sniffed. "That's what I take if you bleed a word of this."

He nodded, his jaw rigid. Like the string of a bow pulled tight. Silence stretched between them, the tension in the room making Sally's heart pound double time. Something seethed in the air. Something that could only be described as sadness and desire. Like an imminent explosion ticking down to zero.

"Aw, fuck guarantees," Rider growled.

In two steps, he'd reached Sally, lifting her at the waist as his mouth found hers in an electric clash of pent up emotion, plying, probing, demolishing. Her legs came around his hips as he backed her against the door and kissed the hell out of her.

Holy hot Rider.

He was frenzied and his lips were hard, not gentle. But Sally loved it. Loved his taste, the heat of his breath, and how powerfully his tongue claimed her. Inside, her fox purred and yipped, loving the attention, when normally the animal stayed far in the background. Far away from Sinful Sally's conquests.

Sally kissed him back with the same intensity, working her lips over his in case this was the only kiss they ever shared. It felt like one she should remember. Record it on the history of her heart for posterity.

His hand slipped up her ribs, coming to a rest

over the mound of her breast. Her nipple pearled against the squeeze of his palm, so hard she knew he could feel it through her shirt. A moan slipped from her throat but it felt good, so she didn't regret it.

Can't regret this.

There would be time later for regrets, but right now, she was going to drink in all of Rider that she could.

He broke away, stormy mocha eyes staring into hers.

"Everything you've done, I get it. I get your reasons. You did what you thought you needed to do, to keep yourself and others safe. It was a badass fucking attempt. But Sally, baby... you didn't succeed. You didn't make yourself unworthy."

She felt herself crumbling to bits. He was tearing her down. Swear to fucking god, if he didn't mean the things he was saying...

A whimper climbed her throat but she clamped it down with a swallow. Only to have her fox get close to the surface. The animal was all press-your-face-to-the-glass excited. Yipping and bouncing. Her eyes must be barely human right now.

"I know because..." Rider's voice went deep, hitting her right between her quivering legs. Right in the core of her heart. "I'd fight every fox fucker in the country to keep you from feeling like this. Like you aren't good enough. It's bullshit, Sally. Feel me? You deserve the world. Everything. Anything. You deserve to be happy. And if you think..."

He pressed his forehead to hers, breathing shallow. Like he was scared to death. She buried her fingers in his hair to keep him there. How long could she keep him?

"If you think I can do that, make you happy. Then I'm willing to try. Just... give me time, yeah? Give me time to get my head straight."

She realized her breath was the same. Shallow with fear. What were they doing? This was crazy.

But it felt so wonderful.

Oh, she was in so much trouble with him.

"Okay," she whispered, shaking all to hell. "I can do that."

How could she say no to the first man to make her feel like she was worth something. The truth was in his eyes, strong and pure. He meant what he said. At least for now. For this moment in time, he saw her value. And it was almost more than she could handle.

You'd better not ruin me, Rider Daley.

His nuts were on the line.

FIVE

Rider was shaking. *Shaking*. Fuck. Whether from fear or desire, he couldn't tell, and both of those emotions felt like they were swallowing him whole. Like he was the tiniest fish in the ocean, and this thing with Sally—these feelings that sunk their claws deeper into his heart than he had realized—was too big.

Shit. She was important. It happened, and there was no pretending she wasn't. He'd been doing that for a while now already. But lying to himself wasn't what he was about.

So now he had to *deal* with it. Deal with the

fact that this woman had wrapped herself around his goddamn heart. It was the reason he couldn't find anyone at the bar last night. His goddamn heart... the sensitive fucking bastard... wouldn't let him.

Even more so because now he'd seen the real her. The secret her. The deep parts she never showed anybody.

And fucking hell, he remembered holding her hand last night. Couldn't remember anything else. Not the stars, not the falls, not the bike ride. Just holding Sally's hand, and the fact that it didn't hurt. It didn't bring memories of Evie flooding back.

He picked it up now, watching as his trembling fingers threaded with hers, and he pressed their palms together.

How. How was he going to do this? How could he be what she needed when he was scared shitless of any commitment. He needed guarantees, but he couldn't offer her any either.

He was so fucked up.

Sally's legs tightened around his waist, and desire flooded back. Her body was so soft and delicious pressed against him. He could take her now, right here. Probably should. He was better at communicating through sex than he was at opening up. But he'd already done a little of that.

And it helped.

Goddamn it, it actually helped. Who would have guessed?

He drew in a breath and even his chest trembled. He stared at his hand interlocked with Sally's.

"Her name was Evie. We were high school sweethearts. I loved her. Good enough to marry her. Good enough I wasn't ever going to be with anyone else. Only wanted her. We had a good fucking life. I was happy. Thought she was too. She left without saying goodbye."

Halfway there. If they were serious about taking this further, he had to tell Sally everything.

"She was gone two whole fucking weeks. I tore my hair out looking for her. Called everyone we knew. Then one day, I got a letter in the mail. She said she wanted 'more than Cedar Valley had to offer'. She'd gone to..." A humorless laugh crawled from his throat. "...goddamn Hollywood. Can you believe that? Said she wasn't coming back, but she'd send for her things."

Sally squeezed his hand so hard, his fingers were turning white. He didn't care. Holding her hand was the only thing making the words come out.

"Next day, I was served divorce papers. Day after that, I burned every bit of her shit in the back yard and boxed up the ashes so they'd be ready when who-the-hell-ever came for it. That was the last I heard from her. And I decided to never let someone else mean that much to me. Ever. Until this."

"It's why you don't get close to people. Your wife. Aaron. You're used to people leaving. Shit, Rider. I get it." Her voice quivered, but there was understanding there. She didn't judge him, just like he'd never judge her. They both had their reasons for the lifestyle they'd lived.

And now... now things were changing for them. Like it or not. Scared or not.

"So I know a thing or two about not feeling good enough, Sally. Not *anything* enough. I know what that shit feels like."

She nodded, her pretty throat bobbing with a hard swallow. Rider pulled his hand from her grip, and curved it around her neck, his thumb caressing the dimple at the base.

"Her loss," she whispered, her eyes flickering with her animal. "Hope she at least got a Purina commercial for her efforts."

Rider barked out a laugh, and with it, all the pain of recounting the worst years of his life. Sally did that. Made him wonder what the hell had been bothering him all along anyway.

Shit, maybe Sinful Sally was a miracle. Maybe she was an angel in a sexy disguise. A sexy foxy disguise.

"Close enough, I guess. I saw her once on a *Farmers Only dot com* commercial. It was a special kind of satisfaction watching that one, since she hates the small-town life and all. Bought rounds for the guys that night. To celebrate her *suck-sess*."

Sally's mouth twisted in a smirk. "Karma's only a bitch if you are. Be a peach, and life'll be peachy."

"Is that another one of your Sally-isms?"

"I didn't know I had Sally-isms."

"You do."

"Then yeah. I guess it is."

His smile felt new. Like he hadn't ever smiled this way before. Or at least that it had been a long damn time since he had. "I like it."

They stared at each other, but it didn't feel awkward. It felt like… growing. Like they'd graduated from something painful to something fresh. He didn't have a clue what came next for them. But he knew he wanted to kiss her again. Taste her again. Feel the way the supernatural part of her vibrated just beneath her skin.

The power of Sally's vixen was addictive.

Rider bent to press a kiss to her mouth. But

before their lips touched, a knock to the door stopped them.

"Adam's here," he whispered against her skin. With a sigh, he pulled back, letting her legs fall to the floor.

Some mumbling outside the door grabbed their attention.

"Someone's with him," Sally murmured. "Aw, shit."

"What is it?"

"It's Barb." Sally grimaced, but Rider couldn't see the problem. "She's going to smell us the minute she opens the door."

Rider frowned. "Smell us?"

"We're part animal. We have the senses. She'll scent what's been going down in here."

Rider was still confused.

Sally gestured to his hips. To the erection behind his jeans—it hadn't deflated an inch—and his eyebrows shot upward.

"Y'all can smell boners?" he hissed.

She shrugged, reaching for the door. "It's a

talent."

Swinging it open, they found Barb with a keycard poised where the handle used to be. "Hey, peach," Sally drawled.

"Hey, y'all. Adam says he's here to look at the washing machine—" Her voice cut off as she stepped into the room. Her eyes went wide and then narrowed on Sally.

Rider cleared his throat. "Over here."

He slapped his friend a side-five and pointed him in the direction of the broken machine. The ladies followed them, standing by as Adam crouched to check it out.

"So, he really is here to look at the machine?" Barb asked. There was a tinge of disappointment in her voice.

Sally nodded.

"Told you, *princess*," Adam groused, digging through the wires to find the guts of the thing.

Barb sighed, annoyed. "Why does everyone keep calling me that? I'm not royalty. I like glitter, sure, but I like dirt more. And I've never worn a crown a day in my life."

"It's the pink," Adam muttered, grabbing a wrench from the box nearby.

"*Excuse me*, sir. But no one in this town has ever seen my pink."

Adam froze, staring up at her. Rider stared too, not quite sure if he'd heard her right. Sally snickered like a teen boy who'd just seen his first titty.

Barb tipped her head to the side, tapping a finger against her chin. "Correction: no one *anywhere* has ever seen my pink."

"That... that is not what I meant," Adam stuttered. "I-I meant..." He waved his hand at her haphazardly. "I meant you *wear* a lot of pink. The color. Pink. Not..." He swallowed hard, and Rider wanted to laugh at how he was tripping over himself. "Not your... your... goddamn it. Go away. Let me work."

"Hmph. Go away? *Go away?* You talk to your mama with that mouth?"

"Sometimes," he snapped, but Rider saw the

flicker of interest in his friend's eyes.

"Say please," Barb demanded.

"What?"

"Say. Please. Damn it," she repeated.

"Please, damn it."

This seemed to satisfy Barb. She jutted her chin, spun on one heel, and marched right out the door while Adam stared after her, looking confused.

He shook his head, turning back to the machine and cranking angrily at it. Rider and Sally watched, silent, waiting for Adam's diagnosis. Ten minutes later, he stood, wiping his hands on a rag from the pocket of his work uniform.

"I can fix it," he said, but it didn't sound like good news for some reason. "It'll take some new parts. Need to order 'em. Could be expensive. I'll drop a list with Seraphina and y'all can talk it over with the old man."

Sally nodded. "And how much for labor?"

Adam roped his hands around his hips, staring at the floor. "For the old man… eh, I'll do it for nothing."

Old Lady Hubbard had taken Adam many of her homemade casseroles and pies just after his wife, Karly, passed away. She crocheted snuggies for little Megan. She'd taken both father and daughter under her wing for a time, until they could function again. Rider knew it meant the world to Adam even if the man had never said a word about it.

Adam was paying it back now. Choked Rider up a little. Goddamn it, they'd all been through so much, hadn't they? Each in their own way. But the entire Dirt Track/Cedar Valley crew was stronger because of it.

And somehow, Rider knew they'd keep getting stronger. Day by day, heartbeat by heartbeat.

He looked at Sally, and her gaze met his, softening.

Yeah, they'd keep getting stronger. And more all-right. With time.

SIX

Rider stood behind the fence that separated the offices of Cedar Valley Speedway from the track, watching Rod work the crowd into a frenzy with nothing more than his microphone. Everybody's favorite hometown DJ sat on the platform, trading barbs with Barb.

The stands were nice and full, and Waldo had been completely on board for a friendly challenge before the main gig started. The bikes would tear up the track before the cars had a chance on it. But Waldo liked to stir things up for the racers. Made them work harder for it, made 'em tougher, he said. *If they want a babybottom-smooth track, they can go on over to county. Where the uppities ride.*

Rider spotted most of the Dirt Track Dogs crew over in their section of the stands. Surge was racing later, and so was the alpha's mate, Ella. But for now, they were all hanging around to watch their vixens.

Blister held his little girl on one hip. She had the proper baby-ear protecting headgear. Annie, his mate and Aaron's twin sister... who also happened to own Red Cap, stood next to him, chatting with Tana, a werecat from the Ouachitas. She'd mated into the pack, and ran her own construction crew. Rider had worked with her building a few of the moto-jumps.

Beast, the biggest of the dogs, carried his toddler, Artie, on his shoulders while Surge and Tana's little girl, Gracie, ran circles around him, taunting the boy from below. Beast's mate, Punk, laughed at the girl's antics. She rubbed her belly where it bulged over the top of her jeans. She was pregnant with their second, and just starting to show.

Ragan and her boy, Kit who was just a little older than Gracie, were over there too. Kit laughed so hard his face was red, and his mama looked both worried and pleased.

Rider watched the crew. They were a family, all of them. And they were enough to make anyone envious. He'd always thought he'd have kids of his own one day. But Evie had wanted to wait. He was so glad they had.

He looked over at Adam, where he sat with Megan past the fence. He was arguing with Seraphina while Mac stared between the two of them like a referee. Losing her mama had been hard on the girl, on them both. Rider could have had that kind of pain to deal with if he had pushed Evie for kids.

That thing about unanswered prayers... he thought there was something to it.

Now the race for whether or not Barb would hear her song on the radio was about to go down, and Sally was already out on the track cutting up.

Rider watched her, his sunglasses in place just in case anyone caught him staring too hard.

Their encounter at the motel had shaken him to his core. How fast everything had come out. How much he'd shared with her about the past. How much she'd trusted him with her secrets. Maybe it was like this for shifters. Aaron said once, that when they know, they just know. All that talk about forever, like his friend could just *know* it was true. Rider had thought it was bullshit.

But now...

Well, now he wasn't sure.

He'd decided to take this thing slow with Sally. They had time, and both of them still needed to get their heads sorted. He was taking this time at the track to just fucking breathe. Because if he thought too much about what he wanted with her, it would lock him up with all those old insecurities.

The bastard past. He'd find a way to put it behind him somehow.

Evie. She was gone from his life. Now he wanted her gone from the dark recesses of his heart. She had no right to it anymore.

Sally revved her bike, sending the crowd roaring at the *braaapp braaapp* of the engine.

"Whewwwww, baby!" Rod howled over the speakers. "Hear that, Princess Barb? You don't stand a chance out there tonight. I hope your little princess tears don't make tracks in the dirt down your cheeks."

Barb nodded, jaw cocked in a shit-eating grin. "The only one leaving this place crying will be you Hot Broad Turner, when you have to play that anthem of patriotic love-lotion on the radio tomorrow. I love my Sinful Sally…" She bumped a fist to her chest and held it out to the track. "…but let's just be real. I'm winning this. This is happening. And Cedar Valley is hashtag *lurving* it." She did a fake mic drop and that dumbass chicken dance she liked to do with her arms.

Rider smiled in spite of himself.

"What do you think?" Waldo asked coming up

beside him and resting his meaty arms along the fence. The man was like a father to Rider. Had raised him after his parents died in the forest fire of '94. "Think ol' Barbie'll win her bet?"

"Naw. Sally's got this one. Sure thing."

Rider looked over and caught his uncle's raised eyebrow. "That right?"

Rider nodded.

"Well, I gotta put my money on Barb. I always did like that old song she's fightin' for." He whistled an offkey chorus of *God Bless the USA*, making Rider cringe.

Yeah, Uncle Waldo's tone-deaf whistling brought him back to childhood. The man had done good by him. Been the best father figure he could. And now Rider helped him at the track whenever he needed it.

There was true love there.

Even if the two never hugged it out.

"Damn, uncle," Rider drawled, pretending he didn't love hearing him sound so lighthearted. "That song's old as fuck. Older than the fossils of your caveman granddad."

"What are you saying?"

"I'm saying you might be old if you like a song older than the dirt underneath this track. I think you're creeping up on old-geezer territory. Gotta get you a cane. Some geriatric vitamins. What else? Let's make a list."

"Now listen here, boy. There ain't a goddamn thing wrong with agin', ya hear? You think you got a lotta time, but da'shit flies by..." Waldo started, but he caught Rider's smirk. "Aw, you're teasing, ain't ya? Been a long time since my boy felt like teasing. What's gotten into ya anyway?"

Rider sighed, staring back out at Sally. "Can't say, uncle. Just feeling like things are changing, that's all."

Waldo grunted. "Yeah. Well, good."

The siren announcing things were about to start on the track blared overhead and Rider felt the familiar adrenaline rushing through his veins. He loved race day. Always had. He was raised a racer, and it helped keep him sane during some of the worst times of his life.

Rod's voice could barely be heard over the rumble of engines prepping for what would come after the bet was settled. "Awright. Here it is, folks. Five laps flat. No tricks."

Those would come later when the vixens took their bikes to the jumps Rider and Waldo had built for them. Those ladies could really wow the crowd out there. Motocross was their element, though they got the asses off the seats for flat track racing too.

"First one to the finish line wins. No do-overs. No whining. This settles it once and for all. Y'all ready for this?" Rod held his microphone toward the crowd, but they were loud enough already. "Awright, then. Let's go. Ladies, you ready?"

Sally and Barb revved their engines, poised at the start.

"May the best woman win tonight," Rod called. "And may it be the one racing for me and the reputation of classic rock all over the world. Amen." He nodded to the track official, and the five second warning was given.

When the go-flag went up, the vixens were off, spitting dirt and mud in all directions. So much of it you couldn't see them for a solid twenty yards. Rider gripped the fence as they hammered it down the straight, looking like they wouldn't slow enough to round the first turn.

But they made it, both riders kicking their inside leg out to keep their balance as their bikes leaned so close to the ground it seemed like they'd tip. Sally dug a rut deep enough to get lost in and then came out ahead on the next straight.

"Track's too soft." Rider's voice was lost in the noise, but Waldo must have come to the same conclusion because his frown took up his entire face.

On the second turn, Barb cut Sally off on the inside, sneaking into the lead and spraying enough dirt at her she had to peel a layer off her mask just to be able to see.

They zoomed past Rider and he could feel their wind even though they were quite a distance away. On the straight, they grinded past Rod where he was furiously shouting for Sally to get her ass in gear.

But Rider knew what she was doing. The vixen was playing games. Biding her time until she could rip the victory from Barb's grasp like it was candy from a baby.

He grinned. So like Sally.

Rounding the corner, she expertly missed the ruts forming in the clay. Barb fishtailed, but handled the machine like a pro, coming back up to Sally's exhaust.

"Yeah, babayyyy!" Rider hooted, jumping up on the fence, fists in the air.

Going down the straight she had a full bike lead between them. But Barb caught the inside again on the turn and took the lead once more. Round and round they went, trading places because they were two of the fucking best.

Coming into the final lap, they were neck and neck. The ruts were getting bad, drying in the heat of the evening sun that baked the track. Barb bumped one, and had to slow on the turn, leaving Sally to gain the lead again. The crowd went wild, and Rider's throat hurt from screaming.

It looked like Rod was going to get his way. Poor Barb.

As they went down the straightaway, Sally increased the gap between her bike and Barb's. All she had to do was maneuver the next turn and it was in the fucking bag.

A chill of foreboding rolled up Rider's spine a split second before his mind registered something was wrong.

Sally was slowing down for the turn, but not fast enough. Her body wasn't loose like it had been the entire run. She was rigid as she neared the end.

Rider's gaze shot to the track in front of her, looking for anything that would have her board-stiff on her bike.

"Aw, shit. Fuck!"

There was no path that could avoid the ruts. Huge clumps of hardening dirt were scattered across the entire track and the grooves from the tires were at least shin deep. Maybe more.

Fine for cars. Fucking not, for bikes.

If she hit one...

No *if.* She *was* going to hit one. And when she did, it was going to send her airborne. And not in a way that she could land with some moto-trickery.

Everything moved in slow motion.

The crowd on their feet, breath suspended.

Sally jamming the brakes even knowing it would crash her.

Front wheel jerking sideways when it hit the ruts.

Her bike responding, going ass up, into a convoluted pike.

Air beneath her. So much air.

Bike flying one way, her body another. End over end, both of them.

Her, like a ragdoll. It, like a rigid slinky.

The crunch of metal when it landed before she did. And the sickening slap of leather... body...

bone hitting the dirt as she followed it down.

Rider couldn't breathe. The adrenaline in his blood, choking him up like his rib cage was a vise. Ears pounded with the terrified screams from the crowd. Somewhere, a baby cried.

And real-time came hammering back with a boom he felt in his chest.

Rider jumped the fence, running before his feet even hit the ground. Had to get to her. Boots digging into the mud, heart so full of fear it could barely beat, he closed the distance between them.

He wasn't the only one charging the field— there was Drake and Beast and Lexington and Ragan and others—but he was the only one who needed her to fucking be okay. Needed it more than his own goddamn breath.

Be okay, be okay. Fuck, please.

Panic was all he knew as he pounded across the track to Sally.

Drake got to her first, and Rider wanted to rip his eyes out because it wasn't him. Then Barb, who'd laid down her bike when she couldn't bring it to a stop fast enough for her liking. She jumped off it and hit the ground running, ripping her helmet from her head and tossing it aside. By the time Rider made it to the other side of the track, a circle of bodies surrounded his vixen.

"Sally, baby... Sally?"

He shoved Beast aside—or maybe he just moved on his own when Rider pushed him because the dude was Hulk-huge—and elbowed his way through the small crowd.

Barb knelt on the ground, hovering over Sally.

"Keep her covered," Drake said, "like we practiced."

Through the panic, Rider vaguely remembered the crash protocol the shifters, and all the humans-in-the-know, had practiced. If an unmated shifter wrecked in a race, everyone was supposed to make a barrier between them and the crowd in case they were hurt bad enough they had to shift. If they were mated, it was a little easier. Get the mate close so they could use the mating bond to heal.

But none of that mattered right now.

"Sally?"

She lay on her back. Barb had removed her helmet. Her arm was bent at an odd angle. Her ankle too. Her eyes met Rider's but there was no sign of the woman he'd gotten familiar with in the utility room. They were feral, glazed with pain, and oddly inhuman.

Her fox. He was looking at her fox. And goddamn, even like this, the vixen was beautiful.

Sally tried to talk but only whimpered, sounding just like a hurt animal. Her face flickered, narrowing just a touch, before it was normal again.

"Shh," Rider told her, "It's okay. It's okay. Gonna be okay." But he didn't know if he was lying or not.

"She's trying not to shift," Barb said. "But she's hurt too bad. We have to get her out of here so her animal can heal her."

"Shit," Drake muttered.

The sirens from an ambulance whirred far

away somewhere.

Rider stared at Sally, broken and bleeding on the ground, and his heart split fucking apart. *Mine.* He heard it like a whisper in the back of his mind, growing louder and louder until he wanted to scream it.

Yeah, they were just starting out, but it didn't matter. Sally was *his*. She was the only one who made him want to *try*. Made him feel... good enough. Made him feel... okay enough. And he wasn't letting this take her away.

Fuck that real hard.

They said mating bonds could heal a host of hurts. Physical and otherwise. Well, he didn't know how she felt about mating, or even how it worked at all. But he knew she was important enough to be his. And if it could help her now, he'd do anything.

Any. Fucking. Thing.

Crowding in close, he peeled the glove off the hand of her good arm. He could see her fangs elongating to poke out from her mouth as she panted through the pain. He brought her limp hand to his lips, kissing the back of it. He rubbed it along his cheek, nuzzling her fevered skin.

He wasn't ashamed to admit he'd watched Aaron do this with Lexington. It had looked like an animalistic thing to do. Like a cat rubbing on its owner. Maybe it would help convince Sally's fox they were mates.

Rider pressed his palm to hers, linking their fingers together like he had in the utility room. Her claws were already forming. If she shifted in front of this crowd, they'd all be in trouble. His friends, her family, DTD…

He leaned over her, nudging Barb back, and put his mouth next to Sally's ear. "Mine," he growled, putting every fractured piece of his heart into that declaration. "*Mine*. Understand, vixen? You're going to be mine, and that means I'm fixing you. You can thank me later."

"That… Rider, that's not how it works," Barb said carefully. "Her fox chooses her mate."

His glare snapped to her. "Don't give a *fuck*

how it works." But Sally squeezed his hand, grabbing his attention again.

She tried to talk, her stilted breath not letting her, but she nodded instead. Barely more than a shift of her chin, but it was enough to encourage him to keep trying.

"Okay, baby." He brushed her hair from her eyes, staring into those foxy orbs like his life depended on this working.

Hell... it did. That was the realization he'd had running over here.

Nothing like a catastrophe to make your heart realize it was wasting time.

Rider cradled his hands around Sally's face, holding her gaze and letting her see everything he was feeling right through the window of his eyes.

"I see your fox, Sally," he whispered, "and she's... *amazing*, the way she's trying to heal you. And you know, I think she likes me."

His face inched closer and closer to hers. Tears leaked from the corners of her eyes, falling into the dirt beneath her head.

"I know it hurts, baby..." he breathed, shuddering with so many emotions, it felt like there was no way they could all be his. "I know, I know it does. Tell me when it gets better."

He pressed a careful kiss to her lips. This had to work.

He did it again. And again, licking at her mouth where she panted for relief. He kissed her countless more times, letting everything around them fall away. It was just him and a werefox he needed to convince that he was *the one*.

And maybe it was him hoping, but he was sure something moved between them. His insides quarreled, nervous as fuck for what he was sensing. Something different than he'd ever experienced.

Like Sally was open to him. Like he could see inside her heart and could feel her... *sense* her presence inside of his.

And it didn't feel altogether pleasant. No, it stole his breath and cramped his middle. It fucking hurt. Why did it hurt?

He kissed her harder, this time feeling her respond. Her lips moved against his now, her tongue flicking. Slow. Careful. But there nonetheless. He felt her fang snag his lip, but he didn't let up. Not now.

A soft rumble vibrated between them. Purring. His fox was purring.

Rider wanted to cry with relief. Wanted to do Barb's stupid little chicken dance. But he kept his mouth pressed to Sally's, afraid to stop, and never wanting to anyway. Because even if opening like this hurt, it was better than anything he'd felt in his life.

"Holy shit," he heard Barb murmur. "It's working. Get her boots off, the ankle needs straightening before it starts to heal. Careful, Lex. Yeah, just slide it off."

"I brought the back-up clothes in case she shifts." Seraphina's voice came from behind him.

"Open her jacket too," Ragan added, her voice wobbling. "They need more contact."

Barb worked Sally's leather open, but Rider

focused on their connection. The purr. The feel of her.

The... bond.

This was the mating bond growing between them. And if this was what Aaron had felt with Lexington, then it was no wonder he was a changed man.

"Ragan's right, Rider. Run your hands over her body. This is going to hurt like a dirty-bitch before it gets better. Sally, hang in there. Badassing the hell outta this one, girl."

Rider started at her neck, moving his hand slowly over her jaw, across her sternum. Sally tensed, crying into his mouth and he jerked back. Her eyes had gone completely foxy. Her fangs had grown longer. Her claws sharper.

She was partially turned. Shit.

"It's okay, *mate*," she garbled, her voice not altogether human.

"Keep going," Barb urged him. "Her wounds are healing, and I can tell you it's painful. But it will get better."

Okay. Shit, okay.

"Hold on, baby," he whispered, dropping kisses to her cheek while he ran his touch along her broken arm. Feeling her flinch under him made him want to rip his heart out and hand it to her. God, it was hers now. If she ruined it, he'd just stay ruined forever.

Pathetic? Maybe.

Did he give a fuck? Naw.

"Back..." Sally groaned.

"What?"

"B-Back... up. Can't... hold it... in."

Barb froze beside them. "Shit, Rider. Back up. She's got to shift."

He felt the others crowd around them tighter, but he managed to put some space between him and Sally.

"Damn it." Barb maneuvered Sally's leathers down her legs while Lexington got her other boot off. "She'll need pants if she's able to be human again."

But when she reached Sally's broken ankle,

the pain became too much.

With a small, almost undiscernible pop of pressure, Sally transformed into a small red-furred fox. Her nose and the tips of her ears were darker, almost black, and paler fur ringed her eyes. The same eyes he'd been staring into seconds ago.

Rider blinked at the sudden change but inside he was practically purring with satisfaction. This was his. The woman, this vixen. She called him mate. He called her *mine*. And whatever the hell came from it... he was in.

He was allllll the way in.

Sally the vixen stared at him warily. Like she wasn't sure how he'd react to the animal side of her. She whimpered, pawing the ground to scoot closer.

She was still hurt. Still needed him.

Somehow, Rider knew what to do.

He reached for her, sliding her into his lap and sinking his fingers into her soft, thick fur. She curled against him as he cradled her closer, running his hands all along her body.

"I got you, Sally," he murmured, pressing his face into her neck. The fox smelled like her. Sweet and sugary. Like candy. "I got you."

Seconds ticked by while he just held her, petted her. She rubbed her face against his, the purr growing stronger. He could sense she was growing stronger too. She no longer winced when his hand brushed her paw.

Her tongued darted out, licking his neck, and Rider knew she was going to be okay. She might need to rest and recuperate, but his vixen was going to be fine.

And so would everyone else.

If he could get her to change back to human.

The sirens were close now, alerting him the ambulance had arrived.

"Sally, baby..." he whispered in her ear. "You need to shift back. We gotta get you standing so they don't try to cart you away to the hospital. Let the crowd see you."

But she kept licking his neck like she didn't

hear him.

"Come back to me, vixen. The faster we finish here, the faster we can be alone."

More purring, more rubbing.

"They're coming," Drake said, a dominant edge to his voice. "Come on, Rider. Get your girl to change."

But Rider didn't have to do anything. In the next breath, Sally had shifted. She lay naked in his arms breathing heavily and glaring at Drake.

"Are you in pain?" Rider asked, looking her body over and finding half healed bruises spattering every part of her skin he could see.

"Not much." Her voice shook when she answered, and she sounded pissed as hell.

"Let's get you dressed."

Seraphina tossed her a tank top, and she pulled it over her head. Rider yanked it down to her waist as she was already pulling her riding pants over her legs. Barb shrugged off her jacket and handed it over, while Ragan scooped up the tattered scraps of Sally's and hid them under her arm.

They were like a choreographed dance, and he wondered how many times they'd practiced for this. How hard it must be to have to constantly hide who you were from the world.

Rider found his feet, linking his arm around Sally's waist and helped her up. The people around them dispersed to reveal the crowd in the stands, waiting with bated breath to see how Sally had fared.

The moment they saw her standing, a roar of applause filled the air.

"Aw, yeahhhhh," Rod's voice boomed from the speakers. "She's all right, folks. Never doubted ya for a minute, Sally."

Rider walked her toward the fence where the paramedics were waiting. She limped a touch, but by the time they'd crossed the track she was walking steady.

"Drake will take care of my bike," she croaked. "Let's get out of here."

"Sure thing."

Rider met Waldo's curious gaze as he passed, and the old man gave him a nod.

Yeah… his uncle had it right. Wasting time was stupid. And he'd wasted enough.

He was going to take Sally somewhere quiet, and get familiar with his fox.

His mate.

SEVEN

You're mine, vixen.

Rider's words were bold as fuck, and Sally couldn't get them out of her head. Couldn't stop hearing them over and over and over. Not even with her head under the water, and the gurgling of the nearby falls making funny noises in her ears.

Yesssss, her vixen purred inside, prancing around all proud. *Mine*.

Her fox wanted her to get out of the water and get closer to him. But Sally wasn't sure. It had all happened so fast. The wreck, the pain. The mating bond.

She realized now, she'd been feeling it for a while, growing and churning just under the surface. Every weekend at Red Cap. Every race day at the track. Every time she saw him, flirted with him. Her attraction to him had never been *just* an attraction. But Rider's claim on her, right there in front of her alpha, and her girls, and the race track gods... well, that brought the bond busting right through the wall around her heart. Put it right in front of her face. Forced her to listen to her animal and what the ol' girl had been trying to tell her.

Rider is the one. Rider is mate. My human. Rider, Rider, Rider...

He stood on the bank, waiting for her to finish washing the dirt off her body. She could have gone home and showered like a normal person. But her fox needed the outdoors right now. Needed the rising moonlight and the open air to heal and breathe. And it had been Rider's idea to take Hog Swallow Road on his Harley, and end here at this specific spot.

Sally broke through the surface of the water, gasping for breath. Five seconds, and she'd go under again. Clearing her head. That's what she was doing. She was definitely, most certainly, absolutely *not* avoiding the hot piece of man perched on the rocks, hands on his sexy hips, glaring angrily at her.

Nope.

That was not what she was doing.

"Goddamn it, woman. It's been an hour."

She said nothing, gathering her long hair at her nape and twisting it to wring some water out.

"An hour I've stood here and watched you swim, and gave you space, and you haven't said a word. Now, damn it. I need to know you're okay. If you don't come outta there right now—"

Sally ducked back under the cool water, cutting off however he was going to finish that sentence. Being one with the river made her feel stronger. But when she came up for air and saw Rider looking all tough and sweet at the same time... it made her feel weak. Like she'd do anything for him. Ruin herself for him.

He'd never let you, her fox murmured. *Mate is good.*

She had always trusted her inner animal, but it was hard to let go of her fears and embrace what was happening. Could this really be it? Her happily-ever-after fairytale?

Sally didn't have luck like that. She had the kind that gave you a good screw once in a while, but never let you get off.

She took comfort in the solid wall of waters surrounding her, locking her out of the world for a bit. The way the current moved gently over her bare skin was soothing. Like being petted.

Rider had petted her.

Rider, Rider, Rider... mate.

Just a few more minutes. Then she'd—

Strong arms slid around her from behind.

Sally let out a surprised yelp that was cushioned by the river, and pushed through the surface with a flailing splash.

Clearing her eyes, she found Rider next to her in the water. He wasn't touching her now. A glance to the bank where his clothes were, told her he was as naked as she was. He was glaring, clearly pissed. And worried. She could see it in his eyes, and it softened her heart, turning it to butter.

She squeezed her eyes closed so she wouldn't have to see it. Memories from the track, the way he'd looked like his whole world was falling apart... it affected her. It scared her. But it made her want him so damn bad she could barely breathe.

But what if he couldn't commit to a mating. At the motel, he'd said he wanted to *try*. And at the time, that was all she'd needed. They would *try*. Both of them. Just try. There was nothing to lose for trying. If it didn't work, she could recover.

Maybe. Hell... maybe not.

But now, he'd won over her fox. The vixen *chose* him. He was *hers*. She'd never want another. Sally was at peace with that. It felt too right to deny.

Rider however, was human. A human could change their mind. He knew that better than anyone. He wanted guarantees. Well, her animal could give him that. But could he do the same?

"Sally... goddamn it," he whispered across the water. "I'm not going away. So look at me."

The ache in his voice made her eyes come open. And it flickered in their bond too. That invisible thread that linked them together. It let her feel what he felt. Love, pain. Joy, sorrow. They shared so much more than an attraction now.

She did as he said. She looked at him.

He was heartbreakingly beautiful under the dim light of the moon. Who knew a man so rugged and rough around the edges could be beautiful. Was it the way the shadows fell over the creases in his brow as he frowned at her? The way water droplets pooled on his soft lips. The shade of his hair as it fell over his face, dripping water down his cheek to land on his powerful chest.

His arms flexed, bulging enough to let her

know he was clenching his fists under the water. Trying to keep from touching her? Probably. She could feel the uncertainty rolling off of him. He was wondering if he'd fucked up. If he should have kept his distance.

A realization hit her. He was wondering if she was like Evie. If she'd throw him away so easily as he expected her to.

Fuck. That. Shit.

Her vixen snarled inside. *Never hurt mate.*

Sally exhaled a trembling breath, and Rider's hands found her beneath the surface. His fingers wrapped around her wrist, edging her closer. And just his simple touch did wonders to ease her worry.

But it didn't annihilate it completely.

"Talk to me," he demanded low, bringing her close to his chest, his troubled gaze never leaving hers.

"Do you know what you've done? Do you know what you committed to tonight, out there?"

"Forever, right?" he said softly. "That's what

mates mean to shifters, yeah?"

Sally nodded.

"Being your mate means we have each other for the rest of our time." He said it like it was so simple. Like he wasn't worried at all. How?

"And you want that? One woman for the rest of your life?"

The corner of his mouth turned upward. It was a repeat of the private smile he'd shared with her at the motel. "It's all I've ever wanted."

He'd wanted that with Evie. Tried. With her.

"Me…" Sally cleared her throat. "Do you want *me* for the rest of your life?"

He shook his head, a line forming between his brows. His eyes narrowed, his lips pressing together before he answered. "Who else?"

"I don't know," she snapped. "Someone in the future. I'm not a goddamn fortune teller. It's not like I know how things are going to go for us. All I'm saying is… is… how do I know you're in it for the long-haul?"

"I could ask you the same thing," he said,

looking skeptical for the first time. "What does forever mean to a shifter anyway? Huh? And... this didn't matter before, when we kissed. You weren't feeling this unsure about me then. What the hell, Sally?"

"We weren't mated then!"

He stared at her, frowning hard.

"My fox wasn't bound to you then. Not fully. Now she's yours. There's no way out if you change your mind."

"I don't want a way out."

"For *me*. There's no way out for me."

His shoulders sagged and his jaw went stiff. "You think you'll want out. Is that what you think? I told you, damn it, I like guarantees. I'm not playing around, Sally."

She let out a growl of frustration, using her closed fist against his chest. But he didn't loosen his hold on her. No, he held her tighter.

"Rider, don't you get it? I'm a vixen. I won't ever want anyone besides my mate. And that happens to be you. You're it. The only one. And fuck you, I'm not playing either. But you, you're human. How do I know you won't change your mind someday? Want someone else? Where is *my* guarantee?"

Realization dawned in his gaze, and he swallowed hard. "There isn't one."

She sighed, barely holding in an exhausted sob. Finally. He was listening to the things she couldn't get out right.

God, she was so fucking scared. Badass vixen she was not. But he wouldn't tell the others. Even if his nuts weren't on the line.

Mate is protective, her fox confirmed.

Sally shivered in response, and Rider's arms came around her waist, one hand sliding up between her shoulders to grip her neck. Oh, fuck. She liked that. So much she barely held in a purr.

"Maybe that's the point," he rumbled. "Maybe guarantees don't exist. I mean, Ragan chose someone else, didn't she? And in the end, it didn't matter. She was forced to mate another, no matter what her fox wanted. So even with vixens, Sally, there're no fucking guarantees. There is only two people trying their best to make it work. Maybe we just have to trust each other if we want it bad enough."

There was that word again. Try.

"And if it doesn't work? If *trying* isn't enough?"

"You say that like I'm ever going to stop. Trying only fails if you stop doing it." His thumb rubbed soothing circles over the nape of her neck. She struggled to keep her lids from fluttering closed. "And I'm never stopping, baby. I plan on trying with you *forever*. And you better damn well be making the same fucking plans."

Her lips curved in a smile. She couldn't help it. He said such pretty words.

"So when you said you wanted to try... it didn't mean... you know, that this was a trial run?"

"Damn it, woman," he said softly, his lips almost touching hers. "Didn't you listen to me at all when I poured my heart out to you?"

"I-I did. I just..."

"I said I feel hard. When I care about a woman, I'm all in. Done for anyone else. And you're the one I care for. My stupid heart nearly fell out of my chest when you flipped that bike. Never ran so fast in my goddamn life. Never prayed so hard."

"Never?"

Rider pressed his thumb under her jaw to tilt her face up to his. "Not ever." His eyes burned into hers, and finally... *finally* everything inside her went calm. All the worries, the fretting, the uncertainty from the past and of the future. It all flew right out the window, lost on the breeze of his hot breath washing over her face as he kissed her.

He pressed his lips to hers like a promise, and she felt it deep. To her core.

He pulled back, staring at her with those perfect brown eyes rimmed with dark lashes. Under the water, he found her thigh, curving his hand around the inside and sliding up. Sally held her breath.

"This bond did something to me, Sally."

"Yeah?"

Rider nodded, dipping his mouth to her ear, his teeth closing over her lobe. "I feel things differently. Like you're in me. Now I want to be in you."

Sally shivered at his words.

"It connects us," she explained. "Our hearts. I feel you too. It will get stronger after we've…"

She hesitated, not sure what the hell to call it now. This was all so new to her. She might as well be a virgin for how new this was.

"After we've made love," Rider murmured.

Sally nodded.

She'd never made love. She'd only ever fucked. Love wasn't something she ever thought she'd get. Now it was here, and she was…

Rider's hand reached her center, curving around to cup her sex. She felt the dominance in the action. Her fox purred for it while Sally panted through her desire and…

"Are you scared?" he whispered.

She nodded. But for different reasons now.

"Me too. You've invaded me, peach. You're all I can think about. It was like this before. But now, so much more. Tell me what to do about it."

She dug deep to find the bold woman she'd been before he'd wrecked her so wonderfully. Reaching for him, she wrapped her fingers around his hardness, squeezing him from base to tip. He hissed in reaction, his eyes going darker with lust.

"Take me."

"Out here?"

She nodded. "Under the moon. Where we held hands."

His eyes roamed all over her face, and his hand pressed tighter between her legs. "And then you're mine?"

"I already am."

"We never stop trying, Sally."

"Never," she agreed.

It was a promise. And a big middle finger to the skulk that made her think she could never be happy.

She was going to have her fairytale, and not a fucking thing could stop her.

EIGHT

That was all Rider needed to hear. That promise from her lips and the feeling of the bond between them was enough to send his heart over the edge.

As if that hadn't already happened on the dirt track.

At the pool table, flirting her peachy little ass off.

At Red Cap the first time she walked in there months ago.

Fuck. He'd been a goner since then, hadn't he?

Rider lifted his vixen by the waist and let her

wrap her legs around him. His erection bobbed beneath her ass as he walked them out of the water to the rocky ledge that created a small cove beneath the falls. The rock was smooth there, it was open to the night sky, and the mist from the nearby waterfall was sultry with the summer night.

Later he'd take her back to his place and have her in his bed. The damn thing was sacred. He'd never brought a woman to his apartment above the bike shop. Sally though, his *mate*...

Oh, he liked that.

...he'd have her there before the night was over. Wake up to her there. And this time, remember every fucking thing.

Sally linked her hands around his neck, drawing him in for a kiss. Her lips molded to his and her tongue pressed in, furiously tasting him. He grinned into her mouth.

"Hungry vixen, aren't you?"

"I've been waiting for this for so long," she breathed. "Didn't think... we'd ever..."

He captured her mouth again, taking his turn tasting every corner of it. She tasted like hot woman and the future of everything. She was damn near magical. Unicorns and fucking rainbows, that's what she was. With a peachy ass and a foul mouth.

Perfect for him.

He laid Sally down, pulling up on his knees to stare at her. He'd seen her naked at the track when she shifted, but this was his first good look at her. And he liked every sexy thing. Soft curves that were just right. Places for his hands to grip, squeeze. Long legs he needed to get between.

All their shapes would fit together perfectly.

She was sinful with her body all wet from the river. Where her stomach dipped inward water had settled, pooling in her belly button. He reached forward, flicking it so it splashed up on her chest. Dew drops settled on her nipples and he decided that would be the first place he put his mouth. Suck them clean.

The familiar wicked glint was in her eyes, as

if she'd read his mind, this time mixed with something sweeter. But he didn't want to put a name to it yet.

Not yet.

"Don't look at me like that, Sally."

"Like what?" Her voice had gone all breathy, and she bit the tip of one finger in the sexiest damn way.

"Like you want me to eat you up. Because it's making it impossible for me to think."

"We've done enough thinking haven't we, Rider Daley? I think it's time for me to find out if your name holds up."

He prowled up her body, scanning every inch of it on his way up and making note of the places he wanted to show extra attention. The list was very long.

"Oh, trust me, peach. I'll be riding this sweet body daily. Maybe hourly for a while to break you in. Here, in my truck, my shop, my bed. In the shower, against the wall, kitchen table…"

Rider lunged for her chest where it heaved

below his face. He sucked the water from her cleavage, licking his way across until he reached the hard bud of her nipple, and pulled it between his lips. He sucked hard, drawing a moan from her. But when he made eye contact, letting Sally watch him suck... that's when she lost it, bucking her hips up to meet his body.

Goddamn, this wasn't going to be slow and easy.

It was going to be furious and wild.

Just like he always knew Sally would be. The way he wanted her.

Rider released her with a soft pop and nibbled his way to the other one. His hands hadn't touched her, not yet. He was seducing his girl first. Not that she needed it, but maybe this was payback for all those times she'd made him so hard it was painful.

He was damn near there now.

Her hands were in his hair urging him up to her mouth before he was ready to leave her tits. But there'd be time for more of that later. If his baby wanted kisses, he'd give 'em to her.

His stomach flipped and flopped with the gravity of what they were doing. This was real. He was laying down all his insecurities for a future with her. This was his endgame, finally becoming reality. Fuck. He was so happy he wanted to cry.

But then his cock throbbed between them, and he forgot about tears.

Sally broke their kiss, wiggling her way lower, pressing kisses to his chest, down his flexing abs. She urged him up her body. Aw, shit. She was going to... she wanted him to...

"Fuck my face," she purred, tongue darting out to drag a long lick along his cock.

Rider grit his teeth against the moan that wanted to escape. Her hot breath on him had his mind blanking hard.

This wasn't how he'd wanted it to go. Not how he wanted to spend his first stroke inside her. But how the *hell* was he supposed to say no to that fucking sexy demand.

"Yeah..." Rider groaned. Just for a second.

Then he was having his way with her.

On one knee, he planted the other foot on the rock next to her shoulders. Gripping the base of his dick, he guided it to her waiting mouth. It was parted in anticipation, her wet lips driving him forward.

But she didn't wait for him to press in. Closing the tiny distance, she wrapped her lips around the head, sucking him down.

"Shit," he cried, crumbling at the feel of her mouth on him.

Sally moaned, the vibration from her throat making it too hard to stay upright. Head was spinning. Fuck.

Shaking like all hell, Rider gripped her nape, watching her eyes flicker with her animal, and thrust into her mouth. Gentle at first, absorbing every mind-blowing sensation. The suction of her lips, the swirl of her tongue. And then harder when her hands came up to grip his ass, sharp claws digging in to urge him on.

Goddamn, he was going to lose himself to her.

Yeah, he was going to give her everything.

Sinful Sally was about to find out just how Rider liked to fuck when his heart was leading the way.

And there wasn't nothing sweet about it. Only rough and hard. The way life had been. The way life would inevitably always be. But with a happy ending that would leave them smiling and battle weary. Because that was the sweet part. Getting to the finish line together and loving the race so much you wished you could have another go at it.

***

Sally moaned as Rider bumped the back of her throat. What they were doing was so carnal, her fox was twerking her tail for him to finish their bond. She was ready. No further warmup needed.

Rider pulled from her mouth and she found herself flipped onto her hands and knees. Pure lust fogged her mind and before she could get her bearings, his face was beneath her. Between her legs.

"My turn," he growled. His eyes were wicked and demanding. Just like she wanted him to be. "Ride my face, peach."

What he wanted from her sounded so naughty it stunned her still. Sally had done a lot of things, but never that. She'd never used anyone's face like a bicycle. It was dirty. So dirty she was considering it. Mmm.

"But I—"

"*Ride*."

His hands came around her ass, desperately squeezing and kneading her flesh before his fingers dipped lower, between her folds to feel the wetness of her arousal.

She gasped at the touch of his calloused fingers against her most sensitive spot.

"Come here. Let me taste that sweet honey, Sally. I won't ask again."

But when he put it like that...

Slowly, she lowered her hips to Rider's waiting mouth, and his tongue made a long lick up her burning center. She let out a surprised yelp and his fingers tightened around her waist to keep her there.

He licked and sucked and swirled until her thighs quivered uncontrollably and the sounds coming from her mouth were unrecognizable. She was so close to release. So ready for him. She'd never felt this lost before. Until now, sex had been a game for her, not an expression. And she'd played it well. She was the queen of seduction.

But now she wasn't in control of anything.

Not her body, not her mind, not her mouth.

"Rider..." she breathed, her hips rotating on their own. Like she was the car and his mouth was the driver.

"Taste so good."

Rider's whispered comment wasn't for her ears, but her fox heard it anyway. And damn if it didn't make her shiver. Gave her chills all the way to her toes.

He latched on to her clit, sucking hard enough to make her scream. But just as she was about to shatter apart, he yanked her legs out from under her, flipping the world on end again. Her back pressed against the warm rock, Rider hovered over her looking more intense than she'd ever seen him.

Fuck.

Rider all lust-crazy and dominant almost had her coming without him even touching her. He was an eleven on the Dickter Scale. She knew it, and he hadn't even pushed inside her yet. She'd told Seraphina an eleven didn't exist.

She was damn wrong.

"Let me see," he rumbled low. "See your eyes. Mmm, yeahhh... there she is. Beautiful saucy vixen."

"Need you," she gasped, pushing her hips up to make contact with him. "Never needed anyone before, Rider. Damn it."

"I know, baby."

He pulled her thighs wide and settled in.

"Don't look away, Sally. I want your animal to understand what this is. That this is fucking permanent."

"She knows," she moaned. God, it was so permanent it might as well be bedrock. But she kept her eyes glued to his.

And as he inched into her, the entire universe seemed to slow to a crawl. Her breath, his. They stalled as he pressed forward, so slowly she wondered if she'd pass out before he got all the way in. The feel of him through their bond had tears springing to her eyes.

Rider let out a shattered breath as he hit bottom and just stayed there.

"Rider." His name on her exhale sounded reverent.

"You..." He trembled, dropping to his elbows and slid his palms under her head to cradle her. "You are so much *more* than I ever knew."

His thumbs rubbed soft circles in her hair. So careful. Like she was precious.

Rider made her feel precious. There was no better feeling on earth.

"And I was willing to fight for you then, Sally. Now? Let anyone, *anything*, try to take you from me. Then see how I fight."

The tears brimming her lids streamed free and she didn't even try to stop them. What the hell did it matter? There was no hiding from Rider. They were bonded.

Watching her face, he rolled his hips back and plunged forward, stealing her breath again.

Their connection was like nothing she'd ever felt before. A union. Two souls becoming one in the way of her shifters. For the first time ever, she felt like her kind. Like she and her animal were finally at peace. Like if a skulk came for her, it wouldn't matter.

She had Rider.

"You feel that?"

He nodded and thrust against her again. And again. Slow, steady. Hard.

"The bond?" he asked.

"Yes."

Rider rolled his hips faster, firmer.

"Will it always be like this?" His breath rushed out. "So fucking sweet. So powerful."

Sally clung to his arms, her hips rising to meet his luxurious thrusts.

"As long as we protect it."

His determined nod and the powerful shift of his hips sent Sally into spasms as he followed her over, both of them finding their release in a wave of bliss so mighty it could have been an earthquake.

The bond was complete.

Now she would trust, as best she could. Trust Rider to be hers. Like she was his.

NINE

The sounds of the night echoed through the quiet Red Cap parking lot as Rider held Sally on the back of his parked bike. It was a short walk from where they'd parked to the door, and the party behind it. But it was taking them longer to get there because he kept stopping for new tastes of her mouth and to whisper sweet things in her ear.

Speaking of...

Time for another kiss break.

He pulled her hand, dragging her back between his legs where they were propped against the bike. She grinned lazily as he brought her tight to his body and curved his hand around the back of her neck.

"We're never getting out of here if you keep this up," she warned.

He shrugged, closing the distance. "There's an El Camino over there. And an El Camino is on my list."

"Your list?"

"My list of places we need to fuck."

She let out one of her new laughs. The kind that came from deep down. And yeah, it was still the prettiest thing he'd ever heard. Drunk or not.

"Your list can't hold up to mine," she challenged.

Rider raised an eyebrow.

"On a trampoline, against the refrigerator door, on my bike, pool table, the roof of the motel... oooh! On the washing machine after Adam fixes it. The elevator, the stairwell..."

"Shit, woman. Slow down."

She grinned so wide her teeth showed. Damn,

she was pretty.

"You're going to be insatiable, aren't you?"

She pressed up on her tip-toes, kissing him sweetly. "As if you aren't."

"Damn straight," he rumbled, capturing her lips and kissing the hell out of her. He was making this a long one. It needed to last them until they got done celebrating the wins with their friends.

But Sally eased back first. "Being watched," she breathed.

Rider grinned against her cheek. Yeah, her list was definitely more daring than his. "My vixen likes being watched? Peach, that's naughty."

"No, Rider," she hissed, "we're being watched right now."

"What?"

His eyes darted between the vehicles around them. But he didn't have to look far. Under the floodlight and the glow coming from the neon lights of the front, he could see Adam.

His friend stood frozen in the middle of the lot, a few feet away from them. One hand was raised to his hair. Like he'd been about to run it through and hit pause.

"It's Adam." Rider lifted his hand to wave, breaking the spell, and Adam strolled forward.

Pulling Sally to a stand, he called out, "Hey, bro. What's up?"

They slapped palms like normal, but there was an edge to Adam's movements.

"Didn't realize y'all were here." Adam glanced at Sally uncomfortably, his gaze sliding down to where her hand was linked with Rider's.

Rider frowned as she started to let go, but he squeezed her hand to keep it there.

"Just showed up." Not a complete lie. "What are you doing outside?"

Adam crossed his arms, looking between Rider and Sally like he was some warden and they were on the verge of landing in his love jail. It sent Rider's protective instinct flaring.

"I came out here to think. You?"

Rider narrowed his gaze at Adam. Something felt off with the guy. He'd never been the most easy-going. But tossing Rider the third degree was never his style.

"Stargazing. Where's Megan?"

"Stayed the night with Gracie. Can we talk, me and you?"

"Sure."

"Alone," he added pointedly, tossing Sally a scathing look.

She stiffened beside Rider, but he gave her a peck on the temple and she went soft. "I'll wait right here," she said, warily.

He watched her swing her leg over to straddle his seat before following Adam over to the doors.

"What's up, man?"

Adam spun, looking furious. "Why don't you tell me," he snapped, his brows forming an angry V on his forehead. "What are you doing with *her?* With... with... that." He flung his arm in Sally's direction.

"Whoa, whoa..." Rider's hands hooked on his hips. He needed to keep them there. Because if this conversation kept going the way it was, he was going to want to punch his friend clean out. "*That*? Did you just call her a *that*? She has a name. What the hell is wrong with you?"

Adam ran his tongue over his teeth.

"Are you with her now? Like fucking Aaron is with Lexington? Is that what this is?"

"Yes." Rider grappled for patience. "I'm with Sally."

"You want that? Someone like her?"

Someone like her… was his friend actually a judgmental bastard? It was a damn shame some people could only see the surface of a person, and not the shiny stuff they held on the inside.

"She's amazing," Rider ground out. "Fucking amazing. And I'm sorry you can't see that."

"Rider, there's something not right with her. With all of those girls. Don't you feel it?"

Rider let out a half-relieved breath. So Adam wasn't a bastard. He was just picking up on the fact that the vixens weren't quite normal. Drake was going to have to tell him soon. They couldn't keep hiding something like this from him. He was too involved with them all.

"You don't understand, man. It's not like you think. They're good people. Like the dogs. And Sally's the best of 'em."

"But do you *want* to be with her?"

"Yes, goddamn it. Of course I do."

Adam let out a cruel sounding laugh. But Rider heard more to it. Sadness. Concern. Pain.

Shit, what was this?

"For how long, Rider? A night? A week? This is the stupidest fucking thing you've done. And the timing is…" He shook his head. "… pure shit."

Oh. Okay.

He was pulling out the Big Daddy Adam routine. He was the only one of them with a kid, and sometimes he forgot they weren't his. They weren't Megan. And they sure as hell weren't looking for his lecture.

"Why don't you tell me what the fuck is bothering you so we can get this over with and I can get back to my girl."

A cruel smirk lifted one corner of Adam's

mouth. "Your girl. Your girl?"

"Yeah, asshole."

"*Your girl...*" he jabbed one finger at the door, "is in there."

Rider frowned, not understanding. He'd think the man was drunk, but he didn't smell alcohol on him and Adam rarely ever had more than one or two.

"What are you talking about?"

"Evie! Evie, goddamn it."

Evie had been left on the dust of the track when Sally crashed. He hadn't thought another second about her. Now her name coming from Adam's mouth was like a fucking two-ton to the chest.

"She's here. She's back. To stay, man."

"What?" Rider's head spun. Evie was back in Cedar Valley?

What about her shitty dreams? What about that green, green grass way over there in Hollywood?

"Rider, she's in there waiting for you." Adam

tossed his hand at the bar, looking almost relieved. "She wants to make things right. She's... I talked to her. She's real sorry. She regrets what happened with you two."

"What?" He knew he'd asked the same question three times, but he couldn't make anything else come out.

"Look man, you can have all the things you lost. Your marriage, more. I know how bad she hurt you, but this is a second chance. Who the fuck ever gets a second chance, Rider?"

He heard the unspoken part of what Adam was saying. *He* could have Evie again. But Adam could never get his girl back. She was gone for good.

Rider stared at Adam in a new light. The pain and hope rolling off him was choking. He wanted to fix Rider so badly, just to make himself feel better. Wanted to give Rider what he could never have.

A second chance.

Adam swallowed hard and Rider could see

wetness form in his eyes.

"You can be happy again, Rider. The rest of us are fucked. But you… you can be happy."

Happy. Yeah, that's what Rider wanted too. To get back all that joy he'd had so many years ago. Before all the pain and wrongs.

"Don't fuck this up," he warned. "Don't waste it."

Rider nodded slowly.

Oh, he wouldn't. Couldn't waste it. Could never live with himself if he did. After all, Adam was right. Second chances didn't come around often.

He clapped his hand on his friend's shoulder, squeezing, and Adam's brow went wrinkle free for the first time in… Rider couldn't even remember when.

"Good luck," Adam offered as Rider slipped past him and through the door of Red Cap.

TEN

Sally watched in horror as the conversation unfolded between Rider and Adam. She hadn't meant to eavesdrop. She'd changed her mind about waiting at the bike and was heading inside so she could talk to her girls, find out how the rest of the race went. When she caught the name of Rider's ex on the wind, her fox went rabid.

Now she stood, several feet away, devastated and unable to move as Rider walked into Red Cap to find Evie.

She blinked over and over as the tears leaked from her eyes. Through their bond, she could feel pain, sadness. Shame. Betrayal. And other things she couldn't name, all tangled up inside so she couldn't tell what was hers and what was his.

They were too new, their bond too fresh. This wasn't supposed to happen. He wasn't supposed to go to *her*. Never.

He was Sally's.

Mine, her fox insisted. *My Rider*.

Sally let out a sob, doubling over at the waist to keep from losing her stomach. It got Adam's attention, his head twisting around so fast it might've been funny if her world wasn't tumbling out of control.

Adam frowned, walking over to her. She wanted to back up. She wanted to run past him into the bar and claim her man in front of everyone. Challenge Evie for him, like the males did. Call a *spur*.

Fight to the death? Is that what she wanted?

No. Death on her hands was everything she had run from. She had given *everything* to keep her hands clean. Given until she thought she had nothing left to offer.

Rider showed you there was so much more.

There was a time and place for killing, but to win a man?

She couldn't. He had to choose her, like she'd chosen him. Otherwise it was worth less than her fucking virtue was.

Rider changed that, her vixen reminded, and another sob burst from Sally's middle. *Rider knows you are worthy.*

"Sally?" Adam's gruff voice brought her attention back to him. "What is it? Are you hurt?"

She nodded, trying to straighten.

"From the crash earlier? You need the hospital? Let me call—"

"No, no... Rider. I need Rider." If she could talk to him. See in his eyes what he wanted... or didn't want. Then she could... do what?

Realization seeped into Adam's gaze and he stiffened. "He's inside."

"I-I know. I—"

"He's talking to his girl."

Her fox snarled at that.

"*I'm* his girl," she snapped.

Adam pursed his lips. "Listen, I don't know what you and your friends are up to, but I don't like it. Something about you... ain't right. You're not good for him. Rider's not himself around you. Not careful like he should be."

"I make him happy. Make him feel good again. And he makes me that way too."

Adam shook his head dismissively.

"He only ever fell for one lady, and she's in there with him now, fixing things. After all this time, he's going to get back what he lost. And you can't do anything about it. You need someone to make you feel good, Sally? Then keep doing what you're doing. Keep making your rounds through Cedar Valley. Plenty of guys around here to make you feel good."

She shook her head, the knot in her throat making it so hard to talk.

"Not... I didn't mean like that... I..."

Adam smirked. "Shit, girl. I know what you

are. You play too much."

He might as well have just called her a slut.

Sally glared at him.

He. Had. No. Idea.

But she was Rider's anyway.

Arm holding her middle, she straightened enough to see Adam eye to eye, and pushed her chin out.

"Rider makes me feel important. Like I matter. Like I... I... have *value*. He makes me feel worthy of happiness." She watched Adam's expression change with her words. Haughty to confused. "Do you know how much that means to someone like me? Do you have a clue, you *judgmental ass*."

"You aren't good for him," he repeated. But he sounded less sure this time.

And so was she. Maybe she *wasn't* good for Rider. Maybe what he needed had been haunting him all this time, and was in the bar right now saying her sorries. Evie had thrown his love away. But Sally drank it up with a straw and returned it a hundredfold.

It had to be enough.

"I *love* him!" It was her last line of defense against Adam's claim, and she clung to it for dear life. It was the only thing convincing her he was wrong. "Can you say the same thing about her? About anyone else? I... *I love him*."

Yeah, maybe she wasn't good enough for Rider after all she'd done. All the seduction, all the running from her past, all the timidity about a future. But her animal—*and her heart*—would always be faithful to him. And she refused to feel ashamed for valuing life. For using her body to keep people alive.

Adam frowned hard, taking her words and looking like he was a goddamn fortress. They weren't making it past his steel wall of judgement. Hard headed *ass*. Didn't he see it, how she cared for Rider?

Barb burst through the door just then, furious eyes scanning the area until they landed on Sally. If Barb was mad, then whatever was happening inside was exactly as bad as she suspected.

"Sally…" She rushed forward, winding her arm around Sally's waist. "Breathe," she murmured. "It's going to be okay."

But nothing felt okay. It felt like someone had taken a permanent marker and scribbled all over her favorite piece of artwork.

Barb's glare turned on Adam. "You have something to do with this? You bring that woman here for him, knowing he had a thing for Sally?"

He didn't answer, pressing his lips tight.

"You'd hurt your own like this?" she asked, shaking her head like she couldn't believe it. "I thought you were good."

"I'm not hurting anybody." Adam stared back at the bar. "I'm keeping my friend from making a mistake. Giving him the second chance he's always wanted."

Barb shook her head. Sally breathed deep through the tangle of emotions in her gut.

"You have no idea what you've done," Barb said low. "Sally, get inside. Not safe out here. *With him*."

Adam snapped his head back, surprised at Barb's accusation.

But Barb was right. The things he said, the way he made her animal hurt… it was dangerous. Animals attacked when they were injured. She didn't want her vixen to kill Rider's best friend.

Sally moved to go around Adam, not giving a damn that she'd be facing her mate tear-stained and snotty.

"No," he argued. "Leave him alone, Sally. Let him be happy. He doesn't want you like that, long term. Who would?"

His brutal words stopped her dead. They were fucking barbed wire around her fragile heart. A heart that Rider had taken such care to heal. Now it was snagged in ugly words and opinions again.

Her fox couldn't breathe. There was nowhere to go, and the animal wanted out. Needed to run to ease the pain. Hurting so bad twice in one night… it was too much.

Shift. Change. Let me out.

A snap of power in the air brought Sally's attention back to Barb.

"You," she snarled, pointing at Adam. "You say another word to her and I'll rip your eyes out..." She cocked her head to the side, listening to something. "Yeah. That's a 10-4. I'll be ripping your goddamn eyes out *with* or *without* the help of my fox. Ain't the first time I told her to take a long walk off an itty bitty bridge. And this time, it will be hella worth it."

Adam's eyebrows shot to his forehead before he mouthed, *fox?*

But Sally didn't have time to think about what Barb had revealed, because she was about to show it up with a reveal of her own.

Her animal clawed at her chest. Sally squeezed her eyes closed, trying to calm her. But she was hung up on something Adam said...

Let him be happy.

As soon as he'd said it, a burst of pure joy hit her mating bond hard. So hard, she'd almost smiled from it even though it wasn't hers.

It was Rider's.

Happy.

She needed Rider to be happy. Instinct demanded it. And hours ago—minutes ago—she thought she knew exactly how to do that. But now...

He was happy. She could sense it so clear, sparkling through their bond in high-def.

And he was feeling it *right now*, inside the bar. With Evie.

A violent sob shook Sally.

Evie made him happy.

Adam was right.

Sally needed Rider to be happy... and Rider needed Evie.

She let out a cry, not caring about any damn thing except getting the hell out of there.

"Your eyes," she heard Adam murmur through tunnel ears.

She let go of her body, giving it over to her vixen to take care of. The pain didn't ease in her fox form, but the animal knew how to help.

Barb stared down at her, furious and sad and shocked. In the background, Adam sputtered, incomprehensible words falling from his mouth.

"Go, Sally-girl," Barb said. "I'll take care of things. Get out of here."

Go. Yes.

She ran, darting around the cars and trucks until she found the cover of trees behind the lot.

She'd go far away so Rider could live his life. She'd heal. And someday be okay again.

It was done.

Her fairytale had come and gone.

Happily ever… never.

ELEVEN

Rider scanned the crowded interior of Red Cap for the blond hair Evie used to wear. It wasn't her natural color. She'd always hated her red hue no matter how much he told her it was beautiful.

His eyes found Barb instead. She was glaring at him from over by the juke box, lips pursed in a scowl.

Shit.

He waved her over. By the time she reached him, she was pissed as hell.

"Adam says that woman over there is yours. That true, Rider Daley?"

Rider followed her gaze over to the bar. Punk was serving a blue drink with an umbrella to a woman with reddish blond hair. From the back, he never would have guessed it was Evie. She didn't move the same way he remembered.

He turned back to Barb. "Sally's outside. Go be with her, okay?"

"Answer me," she demanded.

"I'm taking care of shit, but she needs someone with her. Now. Go, Barb. And don't let her come in here. I don't want her hurt."

Barb eyed him, clearly not sure. "What should I tell her?"

"Tell her I'll be out soon."

She looked like she was about to eat him alive. Like if they weren't in a crowded room she'd vixen-slap him to the end of the earth.

"Fine. But I'd like to remind you *Sally* is your mate, and you can't just take back something like that. You can't play with a mating bond. Think about it."

With that, she spun to make her way through

the crowd toward the door.

Rider looked up and right into a set of familiar green eyes. Evie stared across the room at him, seeming nervous. But only for a second before she smiled that winning thing he'd seen on the Farmers Only commercial.

He remembered when her teeth weren't so perfectly straight. Back in school, when he'd first fallen for her. The bottom ones had been crooked to the point of sitting sideways and one top one sat a lot higher than the others.

He spent a lot of hours staring at that mouth. Once it would have brought him to his knees. Now... it did nothing.

Rider made his way across the floor. The bond that took up home in his chest throbbed. Sally must have overheard Adam, or maybe he told her after Rider went inside. Or maybe the uncomfortable feeling was coming from him. He'd waited a long damn time to face his past, and he never expected it to be easy or pain-free.

But he knew what to do. And when he was

done, he'd find Sally and let her soothe him the way only she did.

Rider stopped at the bar beside Evie. He didn't bother ordering a drink. He wouldn't be around that long.

"What are you doing here?" The first words he'd spoken to her in years came out much calmer than he ever could have imagined.

She let out a light giggle, but didn't answer him.

"Who was that girl?" she asked. "She didn't seem happy. Is she the flavor of the night?"

Rider watched her swirl her drink.

"I heard you were like that now. Sleeping around to get over me. Looking for something you can't find. Why do you think that is, Ridey?"

He clenched his jaw, hearing the nickname she'd given him so many years ago. He'd hated it then, but cared too much to ever mention it. Now he hated it even more, but didn't care enough to let her know.

"Her name is Barb. And I don't have flavors."

"Barb," Evie muttered, sipping her blue drink. "Sounds like a name only Cedar Valley could love."

"Yeah, we like her just fine. Answer me, Evie. Why are you here?"

She had five seconds. That was it. He had to get back to Sally and make this pain in his gut stop. It was worsening with every second away from her.

Evie set her drink aside and flashed that smile at him again. When he didn't smile back, she reached over to brush her palm over his cheek. "I'm here for you, Rider. For us."

"That right?" He removed her hand from his face, letting it drop to the bar top.

Her smile faltered. Her mask fell away, and the real Evie was revealed. The one who did feel real regrets. The one he'd fallen for and committed to. The one not playing a part. It was a relief to know the person he'd loved once still existed. That she hadn't been a figment of his imagination. His heart hadn't chosen wrong all those years ago, hers had.

Knowing she could be a decent person again someday, if she wanted to... it was exactly the closure he needed.

"I'm sorry," she croaked. "Listen, I fucked up. You deserved better, and I know that."

"You've been gone seven years. You left without a word."

"I know. I made a mistake. I regret it with everything in me." Her whispered confession should have hit him in the heart like cupid's arrow.

It didn't.

"Adam says there's hope," she tried, her voice shaking.

Rider smirked. "Not even a sliver."

"He says you were broken-hearted. That when you love someone that much, you give them a second chance."

Rider sighed. "Not when the person doesn't love you back. Not when the person threw that love away like it was nothing more than garbage. You don't give those people second chances.

Never, Evie. You know why? Because you have to love yourself too. Otherwise there's no point."

"I did love you—"

"Not for a second. I know that now, because I've found someone who really does. And I'm going to make a life with her. So if you're here for me..."

Rider stared into her eyes so she'd hear him right.

"...finish your drink, head south, and don't stop until you reach Mexico. Hell, South America. Because there's nothing here for you. Understand?"

She opened her mouth, but nothing came out. When she looked away, it was over. He was free...

Rider turned for the door and doubled back.

... almost.

"Oh, one more thing..." He'd nearly forgotten the most important part. The reason he'd come in here in the first place. "I forgive you."

Again, her mouth opened but nothing made it through her lips.

"I forgive you for what you did, Evie."

She nodded, tears pooling in her eyes, and whispered, "Thank you."

Rider strolled for the door feeling lighter than air. He'd needed to forgive Evie for so long and couldn't. His heart had been too damaged. But his bond with Sally had healed more than just her wounds on the track. It had re-formed him into something capable of true forgiveness.

Adam thought he was giving Rider the gift of a second chance. And he was. Just not the way he figured.

Rider smiled, feeling finally free of the past. Free to love Sally the way she deserved. He was going to make her so damn happy. At least as happy as he was now. And he had so many years to try.

His vixen would be the happiest in Cedar Valley.

He pushed through the door and into the warm night air...

To find Adam and Barb facing off in the

parking lot.

"I didn't know it would hurt her like that," Adam boomed.

"Yeah, asshole! Every woman loves hearing she's not wanted. Where exactly did you learn how to talk to ladies, anyway?"

"I didn't know she was soft."

"Everyone's soft when you dig around inside. Even you, donghead!"

"Someone could've fucking told me what she was. Does Rider even know what he's been kissing?"

"*Who*," Barb screeched. "Whooooo he's been kissing. Ya goddamn asshat."

"So when you said fox earlier, you meant... you meant an actual fox."

She stepped closer, fists clenched. "No. I meant a wildebeest. *Of course I meant a fox!*"

Adam got an inch from her face, yelling, "A wildebeest would make more sense!"

They were either about to kiss or bite.

Barb gritted, "Oh, I should just—"

Rider whistled sharp and loud to grab their attention. When both heads snapped around, he realized Sally was nowhere to be found and all of their words piled up in his head to tell him the messy story.

Something bad had happened after he walked into Red Cap.

"What the hell is going on here?"

Both of them started screaming their explanations at the same time, hands waving and jaws wagging. Rider couldn't pick out a syllable he recognized.

"Hey. *Hey!*" Luckily his tone stopped them. "Where is Sally?"

This time, they had nothing to say. They each looked at the other, politely waiting for the other to explain. Sonofabitch.

"One of you better tell me where my girl is. Now."

"Adam ran her off—"

"She turned into an animal—"

"He said awful things and made her cry—"

"She was already crying because Rider went after Evie—"

Oh, shit. "She shifted?" Rider managed to get the question.

Barb nodded.

"Creepy as fuck," Adam muttered.

"You shut up!" she yelled. "It's not creepy. It's who we are."

Adam stared at her, looking chagrined.

"And he didn't go after Evie," Barb argued. "He went to tell her he was taken. Isn't that right, Rider?"

Adam's gaze snapped to him, questioning. "She right? You sent Evie on her way for Sally?"

"Yes, damn it. Adam, Evie didn't leave the way your Karly did. She *chose* to leave. Tossed me aside like I was fucking nothing. You think I want to go back to that, man? Hell no. I have someone who won't ever do that. Because I *matter* to her. I finally fucking matter."

Rider watched his friend's face go slack with shame. Oh, he didn't like the look of that.

"What did you do, Adam?"

He shook his head running his hands over his face.

"It doesn't fucking matter. Shit!" He kicked a crumpled up beer can and sent it flying across the lot. "I saw you running for her when she wrecked. Knew she was starting to become important. I just wanted to keep you from getting hurt again. I didn't... I didn't know she fucking loved you, okay? Didn't know it was like that. I thought Evie being back would make you happy again. I just wanted to see you happy, Rider."

"I was happy. Didn't you notice when you caught me with her and jumped my ass?"

Barb let out a noise that could only be described as *yeah, what he said*.

"Shit..." Adam paced two steps away and doubled back. "I hurt her. I didn't know. I... you need to find her. Set things right."

Rider was already halfway to his bike, he'd deal with Adam later. "Where did she go?"

"Into the woods. Use your bond," Barb said.

"And Rider…"

"Yeah?"

"Be careful with her. I've never seen Sally so raw."

Damn it. His stomach sank at the thought of her hurting over the stupidest shit.

He glared at Adam, and the guy looked truly sorry. Rider didn't give a fuck. If it lost him Sally, they were done.

"You'd better hope I can find her. And when I do, she'd better fucking be okay."

Rider pulled on his helmet, leaving the rest of the threat unspoken, and roared from the parking lot. In his mirror, he could see Adam run to his truck, slam the door, and pull out of Red Cap heading the other direction.

TWELVE

Sally crept up to the back of the motel, waiting to shift from her fox form until the very last minute. No point in giving OM a heart attack before it was his time. She let her animal fall away. Let skin replace fur and her claws fade back to regular nails.

Sneaking to the spot near the dumpsters where the vixens kept a pack with an extra set of clothes, she watched for anyone nearby. The lot was empty. No business tonight.

Pulling on her stretchy pants and a tank, she winced at the throbbing in her chest. It hadn't faded. If anything, it had gotten worse. It was the reason she hadn't run all the way to fucking Michigan or something. That and the fact that she'd need her things if she was taking a long-term road trip.

Something's not right. Her animal had repeated the phrase a hundred times since she'd ran from the Red Cap parking lot.

The happiness she'd felt in the bond hadn't lasted long enough to keep her fox running. It had faded fast and quick, and now like it or not, she needed to talk to Rider. Needed to know the truth before she took another step away from him.

She went in the front doors of the motel, stopping at the desk to ask the night clerk for a new key. This was her fourteenth copy, the lady made sure to tell her.

"Yeah. Shit happens when you turn into an animal without any warning."

The lady frowned, eyeing Sally before coming to the conclusion she'd had too much to drink. Stumbling to the elevator helped cement that view.

Inside, she leaned against the wall, pushing the button for the second floor, watching as the doors inched closed. The thing was probably one of the first ever made and moved like a dinosaur.

But just before the doors slammed shut, she heard her name.

"Sally!"

No face to match it to as the elevator started its chugging journey upward. But she didn't need to *see* who it was. She *knew*.

Rider. He was here.

Mate came for you.

It didn't mean things between them were okay. Maybe he just wanted to break up face to face like a respectable male.

She swallowed hard, emotions tangling her up as she hurried to press the button that would open the doors. But it was too late. And maybe that was okay, because she still didn't know what to say to him.

She was embarrassed she'd let Adam wound

her so bad. Sad that Rider had gone inside Red Cap. Ashamed she hadn't been able to hold her fox in. Confused about the future, which should have been a sure thing.

They'd made promises with their bodies tonight. She shouldn't be scared of trusting again already. And the bullshit bond was no help at all. In time, she'd learn to recognize what it was telling her, surely. But tonight was not that night. Tonight the thing was a hot mess.

Sally bumped her head against the elevator wall. "Come on, you bastard box. Go faster."

She didn't like slow things. And that didn't just apply to sex and cars and bikes. It went for elevators too.

Finally, it stopped on the second floor, and Sally stood with her nose practically sitting in the crack between the two doors, waiting for them to come open. What the hell was taking so long? Why couldn't fucking elevator doors just open when the thing stopped. It was absurd.

Her nerves ran wild as they groaned apart,

eventually slamming all the way open to put her face to face with a furious looking Rider.

Sally's breath stalled. Her mind went blank. Her heart went wild.

She blinked, and Rider was pushing her backward against the wall. Over his shoulder, she watched the doors close behind him, trapping them both inside. He reached over, hitting the red stop button to keep the elevator from moving. And then he was crowding her, his hips pressing hers against the wall and his earthy apple scent invading her lungs to make her lids flutter.

Sally breathed him in, letting his presence calm her some. Whatever happened now was fate. And she knew more than anyone, you couldn't fight that bastard.

"I've been looking for you, mate," Rider rumbled. His palm pressed against the metal beside her head. She'd rather it be touching her, but the relief of him calling her mate was almost enough to make her cry. "Looking all over the goddamn town."

He pressed his forehead to hers, letting out a shuddering breath. And then he was kissing her neck, wrapping his arms around her and squeezing so tight it was like he was putting everything back together. All the things that had shattered at Red Cap.

"I needed to run," she breathed, rattled by how he made her feel.

Rider pulled back to look at her.

"Were you running away, Sally?" His brow furrowed and a touch of pain hit their bond.

"No." She wasn't. If she was, she'd be gone. "Just running. I was hurt. I needed my animal."

He pressed his lips together, shaking his head. "No. You needed your mate. That's what you needed, but I wasn't there. I'm here now."

She stared into his eyes, so full and sweet. Rough and ready. Like they always were with her. But she had to know...

"What about Evie?" The whispered words barely made it past her lips. "You went to her."

"Only to tell her to leave. And to forgive her."

"Forgive her?"

Rider nodded.

"So I could be free. The past and all the things before you. I'm done with it. There's only you…" He kissed the corner of her mouth, sliding his hands up her ribs. "…and me…" Her nails dug into his shoulder, hope flooding her until she felt drunk from it. "…and fucking *trying*, Sally. Remember?"

"We never stop trying."

"That's right, baby." His voice was rough and low. His expression was the same determine look he'd given her at the river. Nothing had changed.

"You still want me?" And why was it so hard for her to believe?

She hadn't meant to let the question out. She'd meant to keep it tight to her chest. But maybe that was the part of her that needed to change. She needed to stop hiding her insecurities. Let them out so Rider could shine his light on them and let them die under his adoring looks.

"Aw, peach," he purred, nipping her jaw. "Never gonna stop wanting you. I have a list, remember? You do too."

She twisted her fingers in his hair, breathing deep and letting the shit parts of the night fall away under his touch.

They were okay. They both had so much farther to grow before they were perfect, before the past didn't sting anymore. But they had each other, promises whispered under the moonlight, and so many years to make it work.

"I think this elevator was on it, yeah?" Rider exhaled.

Without waiting for her to answer, he leaned back, grabbing her tank by the neck and ripping it down the center, exposing her breasts.

"I'll get a new shirt," he muttered to himself. "Need to feel you."

Sally nodded, her breath coming harder and harder. She needed that too. To connect again, erase her doubt again. How many times would she need this? Maybe they'd have to constantly be reminding each other how much they meant.

And maybe that wasn't a problem at all. Rider certainly didn't seem to mind, and neither did she.

Pushing his shirt up, she ran her hands all over his chest, coaxing a growl from him. He broke away just long enough to rip the thing over his head and toss it to the floor, and then was back to her mouth, furiously jabbing his tongue inside while she moaned, helpless.

Yes. This was her Rider.

Quickly, she undid his belt and then went for the button of his jeans. He pulled back to watch as she dragged the zipper down and reached inside to wrap her hand around his hard cock.

"Still mine?"

He narrowed his gaze. "You won't ask me that again after this night. I'm going to show you."

He jerked at the waist of her pants, getting them past her ass, and then spun her around so she faced the wall. Her fox purred, loving his roughness, loving the way he kept kneading her cheeks and breathing like a bull.

"Bend, baby," he husked, and she obeyed. "More."

She made her body an L and let out a yip as Rider swiped a finger through the wetness that formed between her thighs.

"You're ready," he confirmed. "Good, Sally. Because I wasn't about waiting this time. Or going slow. Or anything but getting inside you like this bond is telling me to, and making us feel like one again."

"*Yes*, Rider. I need that too. Give it to me."

He ran his finger slowly down the crack of her ass causing her to flinch when he brushed over her hole.

"Mmm, that will be mine someday too. All of you."

The idea had her seeing stars, but before she could answer, Rider lined his cock up with her pussy and in one hard thrust, slammed home.

Sally cried out, pleasure making chills break out all over her skin. She pushed her hips back into his, needing more before he was ready to give it to her.

"Fuck," he hissed. "So good, peach. You feel so good."

And that was the last thing Rider said before he became a thrusting machine.

As he pumped into her, Sally watched their reflection in the metal walls of the elevator. Her man was powerful, gripped her hips tightly as he drove her closer to bursting. His abs flexed, his expression taut with emotion and pure pleasure of taking what was his.

He leaned in to whisper in her ear as he continued pounding her. "My vixen, never doubt me again. It fucking hurt."

She let out another cry. Half sob, half moan. "I'll try," she promised. "Always try."

"Yeah, you will," he grunted. "Because you love me. I feel it. Aw, shit... I'm coming, Sally."

But she beat him to it.

His last push vibrated her to bliss and sent everything inside her quaking. A deep moan rumbled against her neck as Rider flooded her with his hot release.

"Yesssss," she sighed, and his teeth came down on her nape, surprising her.

She kept very still, her animal demanding she submit to this show of dominance even if Rider wasn't a shifter.

He kept up the thrusting, but this time slower, more deliberate, until he came to a stop altogether. Sally still throbbed on him, feeling the aftershocks of the orgasm he'd given her, but they'd both gone motionless.

Rider released her neck, lapping at the bite mark. It didn't hurt. She didn't even think he'd broken the skin.

"Shit, peach," he breathed hard. "I don't think I was supposed to bite you, right?"

She smiled over her shoulder. "It's okay. It didn't hurt. My vixen liked it."

"Mmm, I know." His chest heaved while he caught his breath against her back. "I felt her."

Rider straightened, pulling her to a stand with him, but keeping them pressed tight to drag out their connection as long as possible. He hugged her close, her back to his front, and cupped one breast, squeezing.

His mouth at her ear, he confessed, "I love you too. Do you feel it? This bonding's still new to me. So I need to know. Do you feel it?"

He thrust again, still a little hard, and Sally clenched around him. Through their bond she could feel what he was talking about. The sweetest feeling she'd ever experienced. So quiet it was almost a secret, but just because only she could hear it. It was a song Rider's heart sang for her alone.

"Yes."

He kissed her jaw, holding her so tight she knew he'd never let go.

Sally smiled against his cheek as she realized happily-ever-afters don't exist. Just like guarantees didn't. Fairytales were just two people who never stopped trying.

Happily ever after? Naw.

Happily as they go. That was a true-life

fairytale ending. And she'd take it.

Yeah, she'd take it all the way to the finish line.

EPILOGUE

"Who *the fuck* is after my job around here?"

Sally stood behind the front desk of Old Man Hubbard's motel scanning the repair logs. She frowned hard, looking at the list of requests. She'd started at the top and meant to tackle the entire list today. But the first two—a broken faucet in 202 and a loose stair rail between the first and second floor—were already completed. When she checked the other requests, she found the entire first page of items already fixed.

Looked like somebody was taking over her handy-woman duties, and she wasn't sure how she felt about being put out of a job. What would she do with all her free time?

She smirked to herself.

She could find Rider and mark more things off their *other* list. Their *Places To Get Down And Dirty* list. Their *Boink 'Til You Drop* list. Their—

"I could tell you who," Seraphina chirped. "But I'd have to kill ya."

Sally narrowed her eyes at her friend. "What will make you talk?"

Seraphina grinned, fluttering her lashes innocently. "Nothing."

As Sally stared, the vixen bounced to the music playing on the little radio that sat on the shelf behind her. She whistled along to Start Me Up, making it sound like a pop song instead of a Rolling Stones classic.

Minutes later, the song faded, and replaced with Rod's low drawl. Sally could never decide if it was supposed to be sexy and sultry or straight out of a hangover. Either way, it worked. The entire state loved listening to his show and there'd been talk of syndicating.

Seraphina went still as soon as he started talking. She stared at the paperwork piled in front of her, looking dazed.

Hm. Interesting.

Sally had an idea.

She reached around Seraphina and snatched the radio off the shelf, quickly clicking it off and stuffing it under her shirt.

"Sally, no! What are you doing?" Sera was out of her chair and reaching for the shirt, but Sally twisted away from her. "I was listening to that. *Rude!*"

"It was just Rod. Music was over."

Seraphina crossed her arms over her chest, looking bothered. "So."

"So. I'll give it back when you tell me who's running me out of a job."

"Oh, fiiiiine." Seraphina rolled her eyes. "It's Adam, okay? He asked me not to tell anyone."

Sally went still. "Adam?"

She hadn't seen him since that awful night at

Red Cap. And she knew Rider wasn't talking to him even though she'd promised him she was fine. People fucked up sometimes. God, she knew that. Adam was no different.

But still, the way he'd talked her down stung even weeks later.

"Yeah," Seraphina said. "He wanted to do something nice for you. To make up for being the assholiest of all assholes. Barb gave him the name. He likes it, I think."

Sally squinted. "Really?"

"Mm hm. He's here now, you know? Snuck in the back before you got down here. He's working on that washing machine he promised to fix."

An ear-busting screech had Sally's gaze snapping around.

Barb ran full speed down the hall, the biggest smile on her face, her eyes so wide they looked like they'd come right out of her head.

"Holy-*eeeeee* monkey tits on a mama gorilla!"

She hopped the counter, almost landing on Seraphina and sending papers flying everywhere.

But then she stopped, swinging her head one way and then the other.

"Where is it? *Where is it?*"

"What?" Sally asked, still reeling from what Seraphina had told her and Barb's banshee scream.

"The radio! What else? History is being made right this very minute and we're missing it!"

Frowning, Sally pulled it from her shirt and passed it over. Barb worked with the knobs until Hot Rod's station was playing loud and clear, and then she cranked up the volume as far as the little thing would go.

All of them got quiet, listening. And when the twangy chords of *God Bless the USA* came through the speakers, Barb and Seraphina let out a victorious *woooooooot!*

Sally had to laugh, slapping them each a high five.

"*I'm proud to be an American!* Where at least I know I'm freeeeee..." Barb crooned.

Seraphina's smile spread across her face. "I

always knew Rod was a softy for country twang. I just knew it."

Barb nodded. "Yeah. He said since neither of us won the bet, he was going to do Cedar Valley a solid and give the song a play."

"Awwww." Seraphina practically gushed.

Barb continued. "Of course, he says it's a one-time deal. But we all know how easily he can be persuaded."

Seraphina nodded. "Definitely."

All three vixens went still when they realized they weren't alone. And it was a good thing Barb's song was almost over because all the light bled right out of her.

Sally turned to find Adam standing in the lobby, wrench in hand. His expression was dull and his eyes had dark rings underneath. Like he hadn't been sleeping.

"Sorry. Just checking. Thought something was wrong."

"No," Seraphina assured him. "Those were happy screams. Rod just played the song. *The* song. Can you believe that?"

Adam nodded, looking uncomfortable.

"Knew he would," he said with a sad little laugh. "Rod always does the right thing in the end. It's why he's so miserable." He shook his head, realizing he'd revealed something he didn't mean to. "Never mind."

He turned to leave, and Sally made a decision.

Adam was one of them. Part of their family whether he wanted to be or not. He belonged to Rider and to Aaron. Who'd mated in. That meant he was family. Just like Rod was, just like DTD was. And if they were ever going to move forward, if Rider was ever going to have his buddy back... she needed to get that ball rolling.

She followed him to the utility room, leaning against the door jamb where he'd propped it open. He was deep in the machine, fixing the thing for OM like he'd promised.

Sally cleared her throat, and he jerked back, knocking his head on the top.

"I know what you're doing," she said as he

P. JAMESON

came to a stand, wiping his hands on a rag.

"What's that?"

"Fixing stuff around here. You don't need to, you know?"

He nodded, avoiding her gaze. "I wanted to say sorry, but I've never been that good at it."

She pushed off from the door and pretended to check a few of the other machines. "Yeah. Me neither. Saying sorry sucks balls. And not the good kind either. The hairy, sweaty, wrinkly kind."

Adam laughed, still sounding sad, but this time entertained. "Didn't know there were good balls."

Sally looked at him. "Uh, yeah. Would you like me to describe them? Or have you seen Rider's already?"

His eyes went round. "You can skip all that. I get the picture."

She whistled low. "Good. Because *that* would have been awkward."

"Right."

Silence settled between them, but Sally was

patient.

Adam looked away. "You're good for him. I can see that now. Real good for him. Never seen him smile like he does with you. And... I mean *never*, Sally."

"I want to always be good for him, you know. But he taught me there are no guarantees. Don't mean I won't try my best though. You can bet on that and win."

Adam nodded, wiping invisible grease from his hands. "Been doing a lot of thinking. Things seem real clear to me now, and I don't know if that's a good thing or not. Because it's keeping me up at night and making me a fucking zombie. But..."

He found her eyes and locked on, telling her what he was about to say was important.

"That shit at Red Cap... the things I said to you... that had nothing to do with you, and everything to do with *me*. Now, I'm saying sorry here, Sally. But I know it doesn't take any of that back. The least I can do is explain."

Her brow furrowed. "I'm listening."

"When I saw Evie in town and she said she was back, all I saw was a chance for Rider to start over. Be whole again. She took so damn much of him when she left. Just as much as my Karly did. And all I could see was this... *chance to go backwards*. To have what he had before. Because I'd give fucking anything to have that chance myself. And here it was, for him. See, that's where I messed up. Rider didn't want to go backwards. He wanted to move forward with you. With someone who cared for him. I... *I was the one* looking behind me, so damn attached to the past. But Karly is gone. She's... dead. I can't go back and hold her again."

His voice shook and he raked a hand through his hair. Sally could feel his despair right in her center. She couldn't hold what he'd done against him. Not when he'd had it as rough as any of them.

People fuck up.

And people forgive.

Thus is the circle of life. Or was that the circle

of love?

"Thing is," he continued. "You were collateral damage in my storm of bullshit. It wasn't right. And I want to say again, I'm sorry. I don't think bad things about you, Sally. I think if you can pull Rider together and make him smile again… that's fucking good enough for me. That's all I want for any of my friends."

He stared at her, shoulders back, waiting for her judgement. But he wouldn't find it with her.

Barb maybe. She looked like she was holding a grudge.

But not Sally.

"Okay," she nodded. "I'll tell ya what. You quit doing all my work around here, and I'll forgive you. Don't want OM thinking I'm lazy. Or worse, that I'm sleeping with you for favors. He's got ideas about me, you know."

Adam laughed. Even less sad than the last time. "Shit, he does not. He told me you and Rider were married. Said he was mad you eloped."

Sally tsked. "That man. I told him we were

mated. Not married. Big difference."

"Yeah?" He raised an eyebrow in question. "How does that work?"

Sally strolled to the door. "I'll save that one for Rider to explain."

"Hm. Unlike you, he hasn't forgiven me yet."

She grinned, and Adam's shoulders relaxed even more. So much guilt, that one carried. She was confident he'd find a way to get past his past. Just like she did. Just like Rider did.

"You said it yourself, Evie wrecked him. If he can forgive that bitch, he can forgive you."

"Difference is she hurt *him*. I... hurt *you*. Rider is protective. He won't let that go easily."

"True. But I like you, Adam. So I'll work on him for you. Give me a couple hours."

With a wink, she strolled out of the utility room...

To find Rider propped against the hallway outside. He'd been listening. Sneaky, sexy human.

She walked past him, her head tipped high, and he jogged to catch up to her.

"That was nice," he said low.

"Well, I'm a nice person. What can I say."

Down the hall, he pulled her to a stop, dragging her up against his body. "Very nice," he murmured. "But I'm still pissed at him."

Sally smiled her saucy grin. "It's okay. I'm going to change your mind."

"Oh, is that right?"

"Yep. Because he's family. And he needs us. And one day, you'll fuck up, and need him to return the favor."

Rider growled a disagreement, and squeezed her hip.

"And because I want to mark another spot off our list, and I wouldn't feel right about it if you were still holding a grudge."

Rider frowned, but she'd definitely snagged his interest. "Which one?"

Sally pressed in closer so she could whisper in his ear. "Doesn't Adam have a trampoline in his backyard?"

When she pulled back, Rider's mouth hung

open and his eyes were all lusty. He licked his lips, and she knew he was already picturing it in his mind.

"Fine. I'll forgive him."

She went up on her tip-toes to kiss him hard and his fingers dug into her hips.

"I'll go now."

He turned on his heel, and Sally laughed as he stalked all the way back to the utility room.

"You're forgiven," she heard Rider say, and Adam reply, "Damn, your girl works fast."

She let out a laugh—a real one, straight from her heart—because she finally had the fairytale of her dreams. It was a journey she was taking with a lot of special people. Some would come and some would go, but one... one would cross the finish line with her.

Until then, they'd live...

...happily along the way.

For information on new releases, exclusive excerpts, and giveaways, sign,

visit her website at:

www.pjamesonbooks.com

ABOUT THE AUTHOR

P. Jameson likes to spend her time daydreaming, and then rearranging those dreams into heartstring-pulling stories of trial and triumph. Paranormal is her jam, so you're sure to find said stories full of hot alpha males of the supernatural variety. She lives next door to the great Rocky Mountains with her husband and kids, who provide her with plenty of writing fodder.

For more information about P. Jameson and future stories, visit www.pjamesonbooks.com or find her on Facebook.

Made in the USA
Las Vegas, NV
11 June 2021